# EMPT ON THE RUN

About a block away from where Rob stood, crowds of people were scattering in all directions. The source of the excitement swiftly boiled toward him, and all at once Rob had a clear view of the cause.

An Empt, those funny little native creatures that could make a man forget all his troubles, had broken loose from its owner and was careening madly down the center of the street. Without thinking, Rob stepped straight into the Empt's path and dove at it, clamping his hands on the faintly moist plates at both sides of its body. And suddenly everything around Rob was sliding, collapsing, dissolving. Suddenly he couldn't remember who he was, where he was, or why he was there. And when the cloud of darkness closed in on his mind, shutting out his panic, he almost welcomed its release. . . .

# SIGNET Science Fiction You'll Want to Read

# Secrets
## of
# Stardeep

by

*John Jakes*

A SIGNET BOOK from
**NEW AMERICAN LIBRARY**
TIMES MIRROR

Published by
THE NEW AMERICAN LIBRARY
OF CANADA LIMITED

*NAL books are also available at discounts in bulk quantity
for industrial or sales-promotional use. For details, write to
Premium Marketing Division, New American Library, Inc.,
1301 Avenue of the Americas, New York, New York 10019.*

First Signet Printing, August, 1978

1 2 3 4 5 6 7 8 9

SIGNET TRADEMARK REG. U.S. PAT. OFF. AND FOREIGN COUNTRIES
REGISTERED TRADEMARK — MARCA REGISTRADA
HECHO EN MONTREAL, CANADA

SIGNET, SIGNET CLASSICS, MENTOR, PLUME AND
MERIDIAN BOOKS are published in Canada by The New
American Library of Canada Limited, Scarborough, Ontario

PRINTED IN CANADA

COVER PRINTED IN U.S.A.

# Contents

| | | |
|---|---|---:|
| 1 | Ghost of a Lightship | 1 |
| 2 | Warning from a Robot | 10 |
| 3 | "Yours Very Truly, Hollis Kipp" | 18 |
| 4 | Destination Stardeep | 26 |
| 5 | The Curious Mr. Lummus | 33 |
| 6 | Of Empts and Green Juice | 42 |
| 7 | Conpat Commander | 49 |
| 8 | Runaway Empt | 57 |
| 9 | Mr. Lummus Insists | 64 |
| 10 | Danger Flight | 70 |
| 11 | "A Touch of the Laser" | 78 |
| 12 | Rescue Plan | 84 |
| 13 | Fight at the Power Station | 91 |
| 14 | Footloose Afraid | 101 |
| 15 | Into the Caves | 107 |
| 16 | The Metal Rooms | 114 |
| 17 | Revelation | 122 |
| 18 | Death of a Lightship | 129 |
| 19 | No Way Out | 137 |
| 20 | Empt Times Two | 143 |
| 21 | "Good Fortune Across Stardeep" | 149 |

# One

## GHOST OF A LIGHTSHIP

The past, mercifully dead almost seven years now, came back to life suddenly on the first morning of the last quarter. Rob Edison wasn't prepared for it.

He and his friends Byron Winters and Tal Aroon dropped into their seats. The gong rang. There were about twenty boys in the bright underground room located on the Life Sciences Level. The boys were busy adjusting their contoured chairdesks, setting the controls on the automatic note-taking recorders, and checking in.

Rob punched the white attendance button inset into the top of his chairdesk. A plaque in a row of twenty next to the large wall screen lighted up. It read, EDISON, R.

"What happened to Jo?" Rob asked. "I lost track of him after we came out of the cafeteria."

"He's sitting up there with the new guy," By Winters answered.

"Where? Oh, I see him." Rob was big for fifteen, with a squarish jaw, pleasant blue eyes, sandy hair, and a nose that was wide and prominent enough to give him a rugged air. He grinned. "Jo the one-man welcoming committee. With his talent for shaking hands and making friends, he'll stand for Universal Senate before he's thirty. And get elected."

Tal Aroon, a skinny boy with a pointed chin that hinted at a trace of non-Terran blood, said, "Anybody catch this new guy's name?"

"I didn't," By said. "Exate told me we'd have somebody new in the level, though. The new guy transferred in because he wanted this particular course before he took the

1

college entrance exams. The course isn't being offered at any other League Homes this quarter."

By tugged Rob's arm. "There goes the new guy's name now."

Rob watched as the plaque lighted up. SHARKEY, K.

The new student had a narrow face and short-cropped reddish hair. He didn't seem to be smiling much as he talked with Jo McCandless, who sat beside him two rows ahead. He was deeply tanned. That meant he came from one of the surface worlds. Rob reminded himself to say hello at the end of class.

In a second he realized he probably wouldn't have to make the effort. Sharkey, K. was looking back over his shoulder at Rob. His stare was direct and not very friendly. After a minute, Sharkey, K. turned to study the lighted attendance plaques. He asked Jo McCandless something pointing to the plaques.

Jo nodded, grinned back at Rob, answered the new student's question. Rob was almost sure Jo had said, "Yes, that's Rob Edison."

Another glance from Sharkey, K. Outright hostility this time. Rob felt uneasy.

The screen glowed a pale pearl. A human tutor appeared on the screen.

"Good morning, gentlemen. This course is Survey of Cryogenics 414. Anyone not registered had better check his program, his eyes, or both."

A mild wave of laughter from the students, even though the tutor was probably parsecs away on the planet where the course-tape had been prepared.

The tutor continued: "My name is Doctor Wallington. As you know, pioneering research in the science of extreme cold began far back in the twentieth century. We shall spend the first two weeks making a historical survey of . . ."

Rob only half listened. He kept being distracted by Sharkey, K. up front. The tanned boy looked at him every other minute or so. He was making no effort to record key parts of the lecture on his automatic notetaker.

As the hour passed, Rob kept wondering about the new boy's interest in him. He grew impatient for the gong. He did manage to make his notes, though. He had kept his marks high ever since coming to Dellkart IV, and he didn't intend to let down in the last quarter. Too much was at stake.

". . . please withdraw your text cards from the depository," Doctor Wallington concluded. "Review chapters one through four before the next session. Good day." The screen faded. The gong rang. Everyone got up.

"Might as well get the blinking card right now," Tal Aroon said. "The lines won't be any shorter later."

"Here comes Jo with the new guy," said By Winters.

Rob had concentrated on lifting the tiny reel of tape from the note machine. Now he balanced up. Actually Jo McCandless wasn't bringing the new student over at all. It was the other way around.

Jo followed Sharkey, K., who was zigzagging fast between the chairdesks.

"Let's skip the cards until tonight," By was saying. "We can draw 'em all at one time. Why don't we show this new guy the gravball court? We could use a new man at left swing."

The new arrival wasn't interested in anyone but Rob. He held out his hand in a friendly enough way. But his faintly slanted hazel eyes were cold.

"I've wanted to meet you for quite a while, Edison. Didn't know you were on Dellkart IV when I picked the transfer."

Rob grinned. It felt forced. "Have I got some sort of special reputation?"

"With me you do. My name's Kerry Sharkey."

"I saw it on the plaque. Welcome to Dellkart, Kerry."

"Thanks. You and I are going to have to have a good long talk soon."

A few students had stopped at the door, watching the curious scene. Tal Aroon and Jo McCandless exchanged puzzled looks behind Sharkey's back.

"Fine," said Dy. "You and Rob have a talk, Kerry. Ol' Rob's after the marks. But he still knows the best punchcards to ask for when they send dates in from the girls' branch of the Home on the other side of the planet."

"Girls can wait," said Kerry. "Rob and I are going to talk about FTLS."

"Faster-Than-Light Ships?" Jo said. "You going into Space Service?"

"Most every guy here lost his dad in the service," By said with a frown. "You won't find too many apprentice Lightcommanders in the crowd. Heck, you ought to know that, Sharkey."

Kerry Sharkey nodded. "I want to talk to Rob about one particular FTLS."

"Which one?" Tal asked.

"The fourteenth. Put into service about ten years ago." Sharkey had a way of shooting out his words in bunches, staccato, hinting at barely controlled anger. "The FTLS I'm thinking about was the third one lost in a hyperspace jump. She never came back. No trace of her ever showed up. She was lost with two thousand officers and crew." He paused. Rob's palms were cold.

When Jo McCandless spoke, he was less than jovial. "I don't get this big interest in FTLS, Sharkey."

"Ask Edison."

"Rob, what's he talking about?" By wanted to know.

"Something personal," Rob replied. "I'd like to keep it that way."

Both Jo and Tal Aroon were startled by Rob's tone. Kerry Sharkey chuckled. There was a hardness in his laugh, a hardness about the lines of his face, and an air of tension in the way he carried himself. Still, most orphans of the Space Service matured young.

"Edison hasn't told you guys about it, eh?" Sharkey said. "I'm not surprised. At the Home on Lambeth Omega-O, I got to know one of the tutors fairly well. Seems Rob Edison got into quite a few fights when he was on Lambeth himself. He wasn't keeping the past a secret back then. Obviously he's gotten smarter."

Anger quickened in Rob's eyes. "I'm leaving, Sharkey. We can talk later—"

"No, right now!" Kerry seized his arm. "Let's talk about *Majestica*."

The name rang in Rob's mind like a gloomy bell. All at once the peace and security of the past couple of years melted away.

Sharkey was right, of course. At his first Space League Home on Lambeth Omega-O, Rob had kept no secrets about his father. As a result he had been treated as an outcast by the other boys. He stood it as many years as he could. Finally he asked for a transfer to the Dellkart Home. By not mentioning the past here, he had avoided trouble ever since.

But now there was real trouble.

By Winters sensed something very wrong. He automatically sided with Rob. "You haven't been popping some illegal pills to boost your learning rate, have you, Sharkey? I can't make any sense out of what you're saying."

"No, I haven't been popping pills. I've just been living without a father for about seven years."

"Where's your mother?" By asked.

"Dead when I was three," Sharkey snarled. "Where's yours?"

The harsh words made By flush. He mumbled an apology for his outspoken question, but Sharkey paid no attention.

"About your dad—" Tal Aroon prompted.

"My dad was a hyperdrive stacker, second, on *Majestica*," Kerry Sharkey said. "He was aboard when she went out from Stardeep."

Jo McCandless frowned. "Stardeep?"

"It's a pretty remote planet," Rob said. He sounded tired. "In the Lens End Nebula."

"Other end of the galaxy, huh?" said By.

"What Sharkey's trying to say, for your benefit and probably for mine," Rob went on, "is that seven years ago, *Majestica* vanished after she jumped into hyperspace from the Stardeep launchyard. Sharkey's dad was one of two thousand men lost when *Majestica* never turned up." In a quiet voice he finished, "The skipper of *Majestica* was"—Rob swallowed once—"Lightcommander Duncan Edison."

Jo McCandless gaped. "Your father?"

Rob nodded. His eyes never left the hazel eyes of Kerry Sharkey.

The classroom was silent. The filtered air purred through the high ventilators, smelling faintly sweet with germicidal agents. A few boys still lingering by the door buzzed in sudden conversation.

They had heard it all.

Well, he'd probably been crazy to think he could hide it forever.

"Tell your friends the rest of it, Edison," Kerry Sharkey said.

Rob stepped forward. By Winters saw his anger, laid a hand on his arm. Rob brushed it aside. "What kind of entertainment does this give you, Sharkey?"

"I lost my dad on *Majestica!* So did two thousand others. You dad was in command."

"My father wasn't responsible for—"

Kerry Sharkey's snort cut him off. "I heard you were always saying that on Lambeth. Tell your friends what the Inquiry Commission decided after all the evidence was in."

A muscle in the side of Rob's throat jumped. Sharkey shrugged.

"All right, then. I will. The Inquiry Commission marked Lightcommander Edison's permanent tape C.D.E."

Tal Aroon, whose father had been a Lightadjutant killed in a launchyard explosion, barely whispered, "Command decision error?"

"That's right," said Sharkey. "You can't get anything worse on the record. But I'd say that wasn't half good enough for him."

In a remote way Rob understood how Sharkey felt—understood how the loss of his father must have tormented him over the years. All the boys in the Space League Homes felt more or less the same way.

Yet most of them never looked for vengeance, or scapegoats. Their fathers had chosen the service even though there were tremendous risks in hurling great craft through hyperspace faster than 186,000 miles a second. The men who drove the ships out to explore and colonize whole new areas of the galaxy knew they might die one day and leave their wives and children or—in the case of boys and girls in League Homes, with both parents dead—create wards of the service. But still men served, and some died, and their sons and daughters got along somehow. Most of them were proud of what their fathers had done for humanity.

Now Sharkey stepped in close to Rob. A light film of sweat shone on his forehead. "No, Edison, C.D.E. isn't half good enough for a Lightcommander who made a stupid mistake that killed two thousand men."

That was when Rob swung his right fist.

The blow hit Sharkey's cheek hard enough to bruise it and bring blood oozing to the surface. Sharkey bowled back against one of the chairdesks. He spat out angry, explosive words.

"Hold on, Rob!" Tal Aroon yelled, trying to step between the two. Rob shoved him to one side. Kerry Sharkey bounded up, ducked in, punched Rob twice in the stomach.

Rob doubled, the breath going out of him. Jo McCandless caught Sharkey's right arm and twisted him aside. Furious, Sharkey aimed a fist at Jo, who brought his forearm up to block the punch. Rob lunged forward to help.

A klaxon blatted, deafening. Rob stopped his charge in mid-stride, skidded to a halt. Jo lowered his arm. He let go of Kerry Sharkey, who slumped against a chairdesk.

By Winters glanced at the lighted grid in the ceiling. He looked unhappy.

Several lenses around the grid had uncapped themselves. Suddenly a metallic voice boomed:

"Students! Identify yourselves by last name."

Rob glared at Sharkey. He called to the monitor, "Edison."

One by one the other boys gave their names. The students by the door had faded away at the first sound from the monitor computer. As soon as By had completed his identification, the computer voice boomed out again:

"You will report to your respective tutors at 1815 hours for disciplinary action. Clear the classroom. That is all."

The grid lights faded. The lens caps slid back into place. Rob straightened his tunic and brushed off his tan-colored shorts. Jo McCandless said to Kerry Sharkey: "You haven't exactly made a great start on Dellkart, friend. We all have too much at stake in the summer exams to fool around fighting."

"I'll keep that in mind." Sharkey's sarcasm said just the opposite.

"I don't owe you any explanations," Rob said to Sharkey, "but for the record, I know my dad wasn't guilty."

Sharkey's eyebrow crooked up. "Oh? The Inquiry Commission thought differently."

"I know, but—" Rob stopped. There it was. The old, implacable wall.

Kerry Sharkey wiped his chin and laughed. It wasn't a pleasant sound. "Sure, Edison. He couldn't have done it. He was your dad. But he did. And he killed my dad in the process." Sharkey glanced from Tal Aroon to Jo to By. "Nice to have met all you guys. You pick some first-class friends." And he snatched up his note tape and walked out.

Finally By broke the awkward silence. "Rob, you could have said something to us before this."

"There wasn't any reason to say anything!"

"Don't sound so mad," Tal put in. "Remember who we

are? The guys who share the same bunk level with you. We'll listen to your side."

Rob was still furious. "No, you won't. Because you aren't going to hear it."

"Look, Rob," Jo said. "If the Inquiry Commission wrote C.D.E. into the record, how does that make you guilty? Even if what Sharkey said was true, it wasn't you, it was your dad who—"

"Get one thing straight, Jo! My dad wasn't guilty of C.D.E."

Plainly annoyed at Rob's tone, By said softly, "Just because he happened to be your dad?"

"Yes, that's reason enough for me." Rob turned and stalked out.

Several students spoke to him on the liftstairs up to surface level. Rob was too preoccupied to answer. His behavior produced stares of surprise. From overhead, thin white light leaked down into the automated stairwell. The stairs carried Rob up to the student plaza.

The plaza was crowded with boys hurrying to classes. The transparent dome that covered the plaza was set on a rocky plateau. Eastward, white crags rose like crumpled walls of chalk. A semicylinder of covered service highway ran between the school complex and the double tunnel through the mountains. Out of sight at the far end of the tunnels lay the city. Dellkart IV was a bleached, cold world under a feeble sun.

Normally Rob would have gone straight to the depository to wait in line and draw his various text cards for the quarter. Before his next class, he would have dropped in at the lower level cafeteria for a cup of nutrient broth at the corner table that he, Tal, and the others reserved by right of being senior classmen. This morning he didn't feel up to it.

He took another stairs down to his dorm level. In his cubicle he sat staring at the small platinum-framed fax of his father on the corner of his study table, next to the reader.

There was a strong physical resemblance between the son and the face of the father, including the prominent nose that lent the man in the fax an air of authority only now emerging in Rob's features. Lightcommander Duncan Edison had been forty-one when he died. His hair had been partially gray. The little ship-pins of sculptured gold shone on the collar of his service uniform.

*Believe in me,* the picture seemed to say to Rob.

I believe, Rob thought. You're my father—that's reason enough for me.

But was it?

Rob simply couldn't bring himself to accept the C.D.E. judgment. Yet, when confronted by someone like Kerry Sharkey, Rob had no real evidence to support his faith. That lack of evidence gnawed at him painfully, as it hadn't since he left the Lambeth Omega-O Home.

Now a ghost of an FTLS had plowed up out of the past, returning from wherever she had vanished in that *other* space between real points light-years apart.

A gong sounded. Rob jumped up. He'd be late for his next class.

He couldn't even remember what it was. Oh, yes. Seminar in Early Galactic Government, A.D. 2175–2250. Taught by a human tutor who had a reputation for flunking half of every class. Rob shook his head to clear it and left the cubicle.

Another student hailed him. Something about a gravball practice that afternoon. Rob paid no attention.

He thought about having to face his tutor this evening. Discipline marks would do his record no good at all. It was certainly starting out to be a bad last quarter.

# Two

## WARNING FROM A ROBOT

Promptly at 1815 hours, Rob rang the chime at a cubicle on the Tutorial Level.

"Come in."

The voice from inside activated the door. It slid aside on invisible rollers. Rob stepped into the small room.

"Good evening, Mr. Edison," his assigned tutor said. Its voice had an odd ring, produced as it was by machinery. The tutor sounded like a frog speaking Unitongue through a metal funnel. Each syllable was carefully articulated, giving the tutor's speech an even more inhuman precision.

"Hello, Exfore," Rob said. He avoided looking at the two crystal photocells placed in the tutor's head at approximately the position of human eyes. Exfore wouldn't notice this, and Rob knew it. Yet, like most other students at the Home, Rob had grown close to his tutor in the past couple of years and unconsciously attributed all sorts of human traits to it.

Robot Tutor X–4 was seated in a contour seat. The robot had no need to sit. It simply took a chair to make the student feel at home. Rob dropped into the contour bucket facing Exfore. The tutor's hinged cheek plates changed position, pulling Exfore's mouth into a new shape at the corners and forming an approximation of a smile.

"Let us review your first day of classes," Exfore said. With a snap the robot pulled a punchcard from the button-studded sphere next to its chair. "You are carrying a difficult load. Principles of Hyperdrive Theory III is particularly difficult as taught by Professor Bool."

10

"I don't think I'll have too much trouble." Rob wished Exfore would get to the real point.

"Yes, but we want to maintain our mark, don't we? You are presently sixth in your class—"

"Come on, Exfore!" Rob burst out. "How many discipline marks?"

The tutor's photocells brightened. The corners of its mouth snapped down. Exfore laid aside the first card. It touched a blue and then a red button on the sphere beside its chair. A smaller card popped out of a slot. Rob didn't miss the red edging on the card.

"Physical attack upon a fellow student is a highly antisocial activity," Exfore intoned. Artificial lids clicked down over its photocells, then shot up again. The simulated blink indicated the seriousness of the matter. "If I may be indulged, I observe that the human race, which is responsible for creating me, is more capable of building control into its artificial servants than it is of controlling its own emotions."

Rob fidgeted. Exfore asked: "Why did you and new student Sharkey come to blows?"

"I lost my temper."

Exfore blinked again. "Have you no other explanation?"

"Look, Exfore, why don't you just tell me the number of discipline marks? I'm sure you've played the computer tapes. You know what happened."

The robot said something which sounded like, "Ahem." Then it went on, "Very true. I merely wanted to hear your version."

"It's a personal thing. Am I required to discuss it?"

Exfore pondered, touching metal chin with a metal hand. "No. You may accept four disciplinary marks and leave."

"Four!"

"You didn't expect that many?"

"No, I didn't."

"Well, then," Exfore continued, intensifying its photocells, "let us discuss possible mitigating circumstances. If I find them valid, I am prepared to reduce the marks to only two." The robot leaned forward from the waist without a single creak. "I have great faith in you, Rob. You are a fine student—my very best, I don't mind telling you. However, you know very well that discipline marks can affect your entrance standings in the two months of college entrance examinations this coming summer. Because there are so many young people in the galaxy clamoring for higher education, a poor exam grade means that your place in college will be taken by someone else. That would be a shame for someone of your potential."

"Pardon me, Exfore," Rob said, just a slight edge of irritation in his voice, "but I know how important the exams are. I've already decided to do an extra seminar tape to offset the discipline marks."

Exfore nodded its spherical head. "A commendable attitude. However, your premise may be faulty."

"What do you mean?"

"You may be assuming that the new student, Sharkey, will cause you no further trouble. I have served this institution for seventy-five years, with time out only for sabbatical overhauls. I know a bit about human emotions."

Here comes another lecture, Rob thought. The tutor snapped off the recorder in the sphere console. Then it adjusted its tone lower.

"Sharkey's behavior this morning was deplorable. However, his motivation is perfectly understandable. He may continue to harass you."

Rob eyed Exfore glumly. "Well, don't worry. I won't let Sharkey get me down."

"Admirable intentions."

"You think I can't stick to them?"

Exfore blinked. "Oh, I am simply saying that we are dealing with a highly sensitive problem involving human emotions. Sharkey lost his father in unusual and tragic circumstances. Rightly or wrongly, he holds your father—and, illogically, you—responsible."

All of a sudden Rob felt his defenses drop. "Exfore, I just don't know what to do. I know my dad wasn't guilty. But I'll never be able to prove it to Sharkey or anyone else."

"Is it necessary that you prove it?"

"It wasn't until today. Now—well, I don't know. I've lived with this thing a long time—"

"For seven years, to be exact."

"Exfore, how much do you know about what happened to *Majestica?*"

"Everything that is in the official transcript. It came with you to Dellkart IV, as part of your record."

"You've never mentioned it before."

"Until today, it had nothing to do with your academic performance." Exfore's photocells brightened again. "It might be well if I spoke to Sharkey's tutor, I believe that's Exnine, Exnine may be able to persuade Sharkey that he is making unfounded accusations."

*That's just the trouble*, Rob thought. *They might not be unfounded.* Instantly he was ashamed of letting the doubt creep into his mind.

Exfore punched a series of yellow studs on the sphere. A humming sound. In less than a minute another perforated card popped from the slot. Exfore studied it.

"This from the library gives a few facts about *Majestica*'s disappearance.

Rob frowned. "I can tell you all you need to know."

"I am sure you can. However, let me put you to a little test. If Exnine can persuade Sharkey to smooth over the situation for the rest of the quarter, I shall expect you to exercise a similar restraint."

Rob was angry for a moment. But he heeded Exfore's hint and kept from showing it. At times the robot tutors could be—in the fullest sense of the word—inhuman.

Exfore perused the card. "At the time of the fatal launch from the planet Stardeep seven years ago, the Faster-Than-Light Ships had been in existence for only about thirty-five years. Their control technology was still in the development stage and subject to error despite the elaborate failsafe devices. For calculation of the highly critical jump paths through hyperspace, a combination of human brainpower mechanically linked to the FTLS computer was required."

Rob nodded. "It took both a Lightcommander and a computer to work out all the equations. It still does."

"Therefore a Lightcommander was, and is, never wholly responsible for the computations."

"Yes, but the Lightcommander is the only one who could make a mistake."

"Computers can make mistakes," Exfore countered.

"Once in a trillion years, maybe, if all the failsafes break down."

"Granted. Therefore, Rob, the most likely cause of an FTLS jumping to the wrong destination with fatal results is human error. Two FTLS were lost in such fashion before *Majestica* jumped off from Stardeep, I note here. There are no other hard facts except this." Exfore ticked a triple-

jointed metal finger against the card. "The automatic Phylex Monitor Station one hundred and ten miles from the
Stardeep launchyard tracked *Majestica* until it was five
milliseconds into hyperspace. At that time, the Phylex
tapes show, someone began to program a course correction.
After that the tapes went blank. Silence. And *Majestica*
was presumed lost in hyperspace, perhaps disintegrated by
the stresses."

"But nobody knows for sure who made the course correction!"

"The Inquiry Commission assumed it was your father,
since he was in command of the vessel."

Suddenly Rob jumped up. "You sound like Sharkey. Are
you trying to tell me the C.D.E. decision was right?"

"Though it is perhaps cruel to do so, Rob, I have re-
viewed the facts to reach precisely that conclusion."

"To convince me that my dad was responsible for two
thousand men dying?"

"To show you that you must not ignore that possibility."

"My dad was a scapegoat! Someone else made that
course correction."

"Who?"

"I don't know. Maybe the computer did malfunction."

"Why do you take that position? Do you have facts to
support it?"

All at once Rob felt a moistness at the corner of an eye.
He fought it and it was gone. He kept his voice controlled:

"No, I don't have any facts, Exfore. I don't *know* that
my dad was blameless. I *believe* he was, because—well, it's
just what I said to Sharkey. Because he was my dad. He
was a good man. A bright man. I remember—"

Rob stopped. He slumped back into the chair.

"How can I expect a robot to understand? He was all the
family I ever had. My mother died when I wasn't even a
year old."

"I know," Exfore said softly.

"He had one of the finest records in the Space Service—" Rob began.

And stopped again. He knew his reasons weren't strong
enough.

"Your loyalty and love are praiseworthy, Rob," Exfore
said. "If I have treated you harshly these past few minutes,
permit me to apologize. I subjected you to the ordeal only
to make you realize that Kerry Sharkey has valid emotional

reasons for his behavior. Those reasons are fully as strong as yours. Neither of you can prove or disprove the C.D.E. judgment. Therefore you must each act with restraint and bury the past."

"Sharkey doesn't show much willingness to forget what happened."

"You are my charge, Rob. Sharkey's tutor will see to him."

Silence.

Deep down, Rob knew that Exfore was right. He would probably have to live the rest of his days with the awful, haunting suspicion that the Commission's judgment was correct.

Exfore stood up with a low whir of tiny servomotors in its trunk and knees.

"Rob, I will reduce the discipline marks on your pledge that you will do your part in the coming weeks to keep your eye on your real goal—success in the examinations. Exnine and I will see what we can do to temper Sharkey's anger." Exfore laid a metal hand on Rob's shoulder. "However, Sharkey's actions whatever they may be, do not affect your responsibility."

Exfore inclined its head to indicate that the interview was over.

Rob realized the wisdom of what the tutor said. He had to keep a level head this quarter. In addition to pursuing his regular studies, he would have to spend every spare minute reviewing all the courses he had taken since coming to Dellkart IV. He would be tested on every one of them. The problem of Sharkey could wreck him if he let it.

Exfore led the way to the door. "The truth is often harsh, Rob," he remarked.

"All the truth about *Majestica* isn't on the record of the Commission."

"You feel that. You don't know it. Don't confuse the two."

Swallowing a protest, Rob left the cubicle. He had gone half a dozen steps when he remembered something. He rang Exfore's chime again. When the door opened, he stuck his head in and said with a sheepish smile:

"Hey, thanks for the discipline-mark reduction."

Exfore's mouth hinges adjusted into a smile. "Rob, you're welcome."

As he headed back to his dorm level, Rob remembered

that he had promised to meet Tal and By Winters in the rec dome for an hour of tri-di chess. He didn't feel like it now. He went back to his cubicle, shut the door, and activated the STUDYING—DON'T DISTURB flasher.

He put his cryogenics text on the reader, dialed the opening page, adjusted the magnification, and dimmed the cubicle lights to reading level. The light from the reader screen spilled white across his face, accenting his worried look.

Exfore was right on every count. He could never prove his father hadn't made the fatal mistake that took *Majestica* to whatever destruction she met.

*Come on, Edison,* he said to himself. *Page one, chapter one.*

After reading the same three introductory pages five times, he snapped off the reader and rolled into his bunk. The foam adjusted itself to the shape of his body. But he lay sleepless in the dark.

And to think things had been so different only this morning! No sign of trouble. Sharkey, K. had changed it all.

Finally Rob drowsed. Dimly he heard a knock at his door. Tal Aroon, cheerfully ignoring the red flasher, was calling to him to stop the grind routine and play that game of tri-di chess.

Rob made no sound. Eventually Tal want away.

Rob went back to sleep. He had uneasy dreams in which he saw a long, shining FTLS blow up again and again.

He awoke two hours before the morning buzzer. He used the extra time to catch up on the studies he had neglected the night before. When the buzzer sounded, he was already dressed and hungry, so instead of dropping down the hall to see By or Jo McCandless, he took the stairs to the cafeteria level.

The great dome was almost deserted at this early hour. Rob put a glass of red zim juice on his tray. He added a plate of syntheggs cooked to his order in ten seconds by the microwave oven. He picked up a mug of hot nutrient and found a table. While he ate, he plugged in his earplug and listened to his notes from yesterday's Middle Galactic Literature lecture.

The dining hall began to fill. All at once he felt someone watching him. He glanced up. Kerry Sharkey was just starting through the serving line.

Kerry smiled and waved. "Morning, Commander!"

Rob flushed, rising halfway out of his seat. He got control, went back to his food. But he didn't miss the way some of the students in the line snickered.

Fortunately Sharkey decided to eat by himself. Rob lost himself in his notes until someone sat down beside him.

"Well, well," said Jo McCandless. "The cheerful hermit."

By Winters took a seat on the other side of the table. "Abandoned your friends, have you?"

"I didn't feel like tri-di last night, that's all," said Rob.

"And did you take sour pills when you got up today?" Tal Aroon said as he joined them.

"Lay off," Rob growled.

By made a face. "I can see it's going to be a great quarter."

"If you don't like—"

Rob choked off the rest of the sentence. By and Jo exchanged looks of dismay. Then By shrugged. Rob walked with them to class but said little.

As he sat down he heard Kerry Sharkey come into the classroom. Sharkey was talking to some other students. Rob caught one word. *"Majestica."*

Angrily he adjusted his note-taking machine and concentrated on the screen up front, letting the taped image of Doctor Wallington blot out everything around him, Kerry Sharkey and his friends alike.

# Three

## "YOURS VERY TRULY, HOLLIS KIPP"

The automatic referee, a telescoping arm that shot up from the center of the gravball court, put the ball into play again.

The ball popped out of the padded pincers. With a *whoosh* the automatic referee retracted into the floor. The light gas inside the ball buoyed it higher toward the arched ceiling. In the stands on both sides of the court, boys from the competing dorm levels yelled, whistled, and stamped.

The random-choice lights above the court flashed red.

"Offense!" Tal Aroon shouted.

Rob dropped into backslot position. By Winters was racing down the court at left swing. Playing forward, Tal Aroon led the diamond-shaped formation out under the ball.

Down the court from the opposite direction charged the quartet of Blues. Rob found his spot, planted his shoes hard on the slippery plastic surface. As forward, Tal had to snatch the ball back into offensive play before he could pass to any of his teammates. Rob watched the illuminated chronometer at court's end ticking off the final two minutes of the game. The score read Blues—8, Reds—6.

Rob felt bone-tired. Usually four twelve-minute gravball quarters didn't exhaust him at all. Tonight weariness seemed to make his legs plastic, unsteady.

Warily he watched the Blues left swing maneuver into position a few feet away to guard him. The cheering in the stands slammed and echoed up and down the court. Tal Aroon leaped high, triggered his suction tube by pressing his thumb against the palm latch.

The tube was banded to the back of Tal's right hand. His arm and the tube were parallel, pointing straight up in the air as his jump carried him well off the court floor.

The suction generated by the tube's tiny but powerful motor caught the ball high overhead and began to pull it downward.

The Reds fans howled and stamped harder. Tal sucked the ball all the way down until it bumped the mouth of the tube. Simultaneously he pivoted. As he did so he turned off the suction power. He whipped his arm down to point at Rob.

The ball followed the end of the tube downward almost to the horizontal position. As the suction released, the ball shot toward Rob and then began to arc upward.

Rob lunged forward. He triggered his palm latch. The suction of the tube on the back of his right hand kicked in, caught the rising ball at the last instant. The ball jiggled in the air uncertainly.

"Fall, fall!" the Reds fans yelled.

With a *whaap* the ball attached to the end of his tube. Rob took the six zigzagging steps allowed toward the goal, moving his ball arm in a figure eight to fend off the suction tube of the Blues swing man dogging him. Flashing in the corner of Rob's right eye, Kerry Sharkey zoomed into position to receive a pass.

Rob slid to a halt, pivoted right. He snapped his arm straight out from the shoulder.

As his arm straightened he pressed his palm latch. The ball shot across the floor and upward in an arc. Rob watched it, sweat dampening his singlet and shorts. The Reds needed at least a tie in this one to cinch the dorm level trophy. The way the arm was snapped and the ball released to the other player on a pass was critical. Rob's pass hadn't felt just right. He had delayed the suction turn-off a fraction of a second—

Kerry Sharkey darted in beneath the rising ball. He flung his tube arm upward, turned on the suction.

"Fall, fall, fall!" It was a steady, rhythmic chant from the stands.

The ball hesitated, pulled aloft by the gas inside it, pulled downward by the stream of suction from Sharkey's wrist tube.

Abruptly the ball shot up toward the ceiling. Rob groaned.

Kerry Sharkey and Tal Aroon glared at him. The automatic referee telescoped up out of the court floor, released a new ball from its pincers. The random-choice lights changed to blue. The Blues went on the offense. They scored their goal in the last seconds.

The chronometer lighted up like a display of shooting stars. Klaxons blared briefly. The final score went up.

Rob's ankle hurt as he walked off the court. He had twisted it in the third quarter and paid no attention until now. By Winters passed him, hurrying to the showers.

"Tough luck," By said. All Rob saw was his back.

Rob wiped sweat out of his eyes and kept going. They were all like that lately—Jo, Tal, and By. They dropped into his cubicle less often. Of course it was now two weeks till the end of the quarter. In addition to final tests, the students had the extra weight of the college exams ahead of them. Everyone was getting tired.

Kerry Sharkey loped up beside him. "That was a rotten pass, Edison."

All quarter long Rob had listened to Sharkey's gibes. After the first few weeks he had hardened himself—outwardly, anyway—so that he could turn them aside. But tonight, with the pain in his ankle, he couldn't keep his temper:

"We all make mistakes, Sharkey. So why don't you just shut up?"

Sharkey blocked the shower entrance, facing Rob. The corners of his mouth curled up. "Yeah, but big mistakes seem to run in your family."

"I got your message a long time ago." With a growl Rob grabbed Sharkey's shoulder and shoved him aside. Sharkey banged against the wall. For a moment Rob's face was ugly. He stalked into the showers.

Kerry Sharkey hung back, startled. Rob's behavior shocked even himself. He discarded his uniform and stepped under the intermixed spray of hot detergent water and skin nutrients, closed his eyes and threw his head back.

The spray soothed him a little. Not much.

That was a lousy trick, losing your temper, he said to himself. What the social psychers would call antipersonality violence. Outmoded behavior. Worthy of the twentieth century, maybe. But out of place today.

Finishing his shower, Rob noticed that Sharkey had skipped the ritual, dressed, and left the intramural area. Tal

Aroon and By Winters had been on the opposite side of the steamy room when Rob came in. They had gone too. Glum, Rob walked into the empty locker hall. He pulled on his shorts and tunic and went back to his cubicle.

He sat on the edge of his bed. He glanced listlessly at his pile of note tapes from the day's lectures.

He should review those. He didn't feel like it.

He wondered whether By and Tal would stop by, as they usually did after a gravball match, to suggest a snack. He wouldn't blame them if they didn't.

They didn't.

Rob puttered in his room for half an hour. Then he walked down to By's cubicle. The tiny light beside the jamb glowed, showing that By had left, but could be found by interrogating the Locater computer via the question-phone at the end of the corridor. A check of Tal's room proved it empty too. Rob didn't bother asking the computer when they had gone.

Shoulders slumping, he returned to his room. What was it By had told him last week? That his whole personality seemed to have downgraded during the quarter? That he'd wrecked his chances of an election to Senior Constellation, the honorary club?

"You growl," By told him. "You sneer. You used to smile. Can't you forget your father's ship for one minute?"

"Sharkey won't let me."

"Ignore him."

"Ignore him when he uses the word 'murder'?"

"Check, check! I appreciate the problem." By had raised his hand and walked away that time too, tired of hearing about it.

Well, Rob was tired of thinking about it. Maybe he could squeeze by the finals with decent grades, then really get down to work during the four-week pre-test holiday and lose himself in study. After all, friends weren't half as important as top marks.

He said to himself several times. But he didn't really believe it.

Finally Rob picked one of the note tapes and threaded it onto the playback. He was just about to slip on the earphones when he noticed the little green message light glowing.

He flipped the green light off and dialed the selector pointer. An instant later the lid of the message chute popped open. An index card with a bit of black film stuck into a slit appeared.

Rob studied the card. The letter, a stamp-size piece of film sent sans envelope, had been forwarded from the Lambeth Omega-O Home by FTLS micromail. Official stamps on the delivery card showed the arrival time at Lambeth eight days ago, the arrival on Dellkart earlier this afternoon.

Rob fed the letter into the reader, illuminated the screen. The letterhead was printed in flamboyant green phosphotype on gray stock. The letterhead said, HOLLIS KIPP. This was followed by a micromail delivery number for the planet Weems' Resort.

A startled expression flicked across Rob's face. He recognized the name. Hollis Kipp was a popular journalist, the author of a good half dozen microbooks. Each one had been a best seller that sent people flocking to the vendalls to slip their cash-cards into the proper slot and receive in return the microcard that carried six or seven hundred pages of Kipp's latest prose.

There's a mistake, Rob thought.

But there wasn't. The letter was addressed to *Mr. Robert Edison, Space League Home, Lambeth Omega-O*. A parenthetical notation read, *Kindly Forward if Necessary*.

Quickly Rob looked at the bottom of the letter. The *Hollis Kipp* signature was a big black flourish. Why would such a famous author be writing him?

Rob had plowed through one of Kipp's microbooks as supplementary reading in a course in recent space history. Kipp did a fair research job, though not enough to be considered a scholarly writer. He presented his facts with a lively style, but was not noted for accuracy. In fact, the course tutor had advised the students to read Kipp only for a quick general survey of the period covered. They were warned to ignore altogether Kipp's analysis of various historical personalities involved in the early days of galactic colonization. Kipp deliberately made controversial judgments of such people, for the sake of increasing sales of what he wrote.

A small cold knot formed in Rob's stomach as he remembered one other thing.

Hollis Kipp's books always dealt with space travel. Frowning, Rob began to read:

Dear Mr. Edison:

Perhaps you are already acquainted with my various works of nonfiction, all of which have appeared under the Solar Press cardlabel. This fall I will be commencing research on my next microbook. I am writing to a number of people in the hope that they may be able to provide helpful background information.

My rough working title will give you an idea of the book's theme and scope—"FTLS, The Early Days, A Definitive Account."

I propose to narrate and dramatize the events of the first decades of the FTLS—the technological accomplishments, the dangers and incredible challenges and—yes, the high price in human life that was initially paid to bring about this fundamental change in travel throughout our galaxy.

A portion of the book will, of course, deal with the three great FTLS disasters that occurred during this period, including the loss of FTLS *Majestica,* of which your father was Lightcommander.

In this connection, I would like to interview you via interplanetary tape-cable at a time and date to be mutually arranged. My publishers will bear all costs of the interview hookup. Your memories, comments, and other information pertaining to your father would be most helpful.

I must tell you, as I tell all those I interview, that I cannot promise to utilize your information in a way that will completely please you. My prime goal is to reevaluate the past with a fresh insight.

Hah, Rob thought. Are you sure your prime goal isn't to malign a few people to get everybody reading your book? Almost dreading the last paragraphs, he went back to the letter.

The Inquiry Commission passed judgment on your father's role in the *Majestica* tragedy. I trust, however, that you will be candid enough to give me your side of it—and that the passage of time has made such an interview possible by removing much of the personal pain you must have felt, even though you were relatively young at the time *Majestica* disappeared. Children often see the truth we adults miss!

I make this inquiry in order to organize my interview schedule well ahead of time, and also to learn
which interview subjects are willing to cooperate.

I am sincerely hopeful that you can see your way
clear to discuss the Lightcommander of *Majestica* as
you remember him.

Please contact me at the above address with your
reaction.

Yours very truly,
Hollis Kipp

Incredulously, Rob once more scanned the closely
packed paragraphs of ultra-elite type. Hollis Kipp was going to rake up the past completely—and profitably—and
spread it out for billions of readers. Further, Kipp would
probably indulge in his usual character analysis.

What if one of his targets was Lightcommander Duncan
Edison? What if Kipp found him guilty all over again?

Rob had a terrible tight feeling in his middle now. This
was worse than the appearance of Kerry Sharkey. This was
far worse. Automatically, Hollis Kipp had an audience of
staggering size. Automatically, the story of Rob's father's
C.D.E. would go into thousands of microlibraries on hundreds of planets, and be preserved there for centuries.

With an angry snort Rob snapped off the reader.

What if he did refuse to let Hollis Kipp interview him in
the fall? What difference would his refusal really make?
Kipp would get the whole story anyway—or at least the
story told by the record books. He'd probably get plenty of
interviews rfom people like Kerry Sharkey!

Slowly, the shock of what was happening crept over him.
He sat down on the bed again, head in his hands. He sat
that way for perhaps five minutes.

Suddenly his head came up.

Some of the fatigue had left his face. His eyes were
brighter, determined.

He might be able to do something before Hollis Kipp set
to work digging into the fatal launch from Stardeep. He
might just have time during the official four-week holiday
before the exams. He had to do it, so he could at long last
confront the Kerry Sharkeys and the Hollis Kipps with the
truth.

New confidence surged through Rob. He felt a little
giddy. The plan's details had fallen into place quickly, even

though it was not exactly the sort of plan a young man his age thought up. Especially not on the eve of the critical precollege tests.

But he felt a lot better for having made the decision.

He washed up and dimmed the lights in his cubicle. He took one last look at his father's fax in the burnished platinum frame. Then he hurried to the Tutorial Level.

He ran the chime. When he got the voice signal to enter, he rushed inside.

"Exfore, when the quarter's over I'm going to Stardeep. And you've got to help me get there."

# Four

## DESTINATION STARDEEP

When Rob started explaining his plan, Exfore's hinged cheek plates changed position and formed what could only be called an unhappy expression. The mention of Hollis Kipp caused the robot's photocells to intensity to near maximum brightness. The glow slowly subsided. Exfore sat in its chair with that glum look as Rob finished. For several moments it said nothing.

Finally Rob burst out. "You're acting like making the trip is impossible!"

"It is not impossible in terms of time. You do have the official four-week holiday at your disposal. However, most students at the Home—"

"—will be studying. I know." Rob looked a little lost. "Exfore, there just isn't any point in going ahead with anything, exams included, unless I can go to Stardeep first. All I need is a loan from the Space League Fund for passage and expenses."

Exfore made noises that sounded vaguely like, "Um, yes," while its photocells revolved in their sockets. Rob stood with his fists tight at his sides. At last Exfore's synthetic eyes came to rest. Its head jerked ever so little as though it were emerging from deep thought.

"No problem there, I should imagine. But, Rob—are you certain that you are not merely overreacting to that inquiry from author Kipp?"

Fiercely Rob shook his head. "This has been building up for a long time."

"I imagine so," Exfore agreed. "Probably since long before Sharkey arrived." A pause. "As to your missing the study opportunity afforded by the holiday, your prefinal averages have remained high. You have excellent recall, so even if you didn't study for those four weeks, you ought to do well in the tests. That is not what is bothering me."

"Then what is?"

"The purpose of the trip."

"That's simple. I want to find out all I can about what really happened to *Majestica.*"

Exfore continued to stare at Rob with that fixed, glum set to its mouth. It raised one hand, extended a cautionary metal forefinger. "Understood. However, what can you possibly learn that the Inquiry Commission did not? Or, for that matter, that Hollis Kipp will not learn if he goes to Stardeep?"

"Exfore," Rob said, "I honestly don't know. Maybe I won't learn a thing. But at least I can go to the Phylex Monitor Station. I can listen to the last *Majestica* tapes for myself, and ask questions for myself at the launchyard. Maybe there are spacemonkeys working there who were at the yard seven years ago. Sure, it's a long chance. And the whole thing's probably hopeless—But I have to do it. Exfore! I have to!"

The robot scrutinized the boy for some moments. Then it turned both of its hands palm upward. Ceiling light reflected from the smooth, shining metal surfaces. "We are dealing here with an area of human behavior which I find confusing. On an abstract level, I can understand why you wish to go. But I cannot summon the same enthusiasm you possess. Doubtless this is because I had neither mother nor father. In any case, my reasoning sees past your emotional need to the various pitfalls. Failure and keen disappointment for you, not to mention—"

"Will you help me apply for the loan or won't you?" Rob exclaimed.

There were more strained seconds of silence. At last Exfore replied:

"Against the dictates of all my logic circuits, I will."

Rob was disappointed. "Look at it from my side, Exfore! I know it may be a futile trip. But doing nothing is worse. If I don't go, all I can look forward to is a life of listening to accusations from people like Kerry Sharkey. Besides—"

Exfore held up its right hand. Rob stopped, embarrassed. "You have convinced me of your sincerity, Rob." The robot's photocells seemed to glow less brightly. "Against all logical probabilities, I will not only help you, I will also entertain the hope that you will discover something new and significant—even if that should be incontrovertible proof that the record of the past must stand as written."

"I think that would be better than never knowing at all," Rob said. But he wasn't sure. It might be torture to live with that kind of truth the rest of his life. He managed to add with genuine sincerity, "Thanks for saying what you just did, Exfore."

Something click-tocked in the robot's polished cylinder of a neck. The sound faintly resembled a human being clearing his throat. "Let us get down to practical matters." Exfore touched a series of studs on the chair-side sphere.

In a moment the sphere stopped humming. An information card popped from the slot. Exfore scanned the card. "You will be on an extremely tight schedule. The light-jumps to the Lens End Nebula total almost a week. Only second-class passenger service is available. You will have to be satisfied with accommodations on a lightfreighter."

Now Rob was beginning to get genuinely excited. "Fine with me! What's it cost?"

"One-way passage is fourteen hundred microcredits. Round trip, twenty-five hundred."

A thick lump formed in Rob's throat. He swallowed it away. "That much?"

Exfore leaped into the opening. "Perhaps you'd care to reconsider—"

"No. No, I can't, I'll get the money from the Fund."

Exfore's photocells rolled upward in its head as it calculated. "Allow another two hundred microcredits per week for expenses while on Stardeep. You will require a sum of twenty-nine hundred. Let's round it off to three thousand to be safe. Provided you pass your examinations and do well in college, your adult earning potential will allow you to repay that amount within five years after taking your first position."

The robot's meaning hadn't escaped Rob. His whole future, including the computer's willingness to grant the loan, as well as his ability to pay it back, depended on the exams.

"When can we apply for the loan?" Rob wanted to know.

Exfore consulted the chron inset in one wall of the cubicle. "Perhaps since it's growing late, it would be wise if we waited until tomorrow—"

"I'm not tired. And you and the Home computer never sleep. Can't we do it right now?"

Exfore articulated its waist, hip, and knee joints and stood up. "Very well."

The automated stairs carried them up toward Administrative Level, which was below the student plaza. They passed student levels, deserted except for an occasional boy drifting back to his cubicle from a cooperative study session. The robot's metal soles clanged on the porous plasto floor as they stepped off the stairs. They proceeded down a long, empty hall where tiny lights glowed behind the nameplates of the various human deans and staff members.

From the stairwell came a sudden clamor of voices. The weekly dipix feature in the auditorium was letting out. Those voices sounded far away, impersonal. Rob realized again just how his quest had cut him off from the normal routine of student life. When he thought about the awesome distance to Stardeep, he was more than a little apprehensive.

Exfore's photocells lighted the way ahead. They turned into a large arch with an identifying plaque which read STUDENT COMPUTER SERVICES. Three walls of the large chamber were taken up with small open-topped booths soundproofed by a tight sonic field. On the fourth wall, opposite the arch, several thousand tiny squares of transglass flickered with colored lights.

The master Space League computer was located on distant Coenworld. This was merely a massive interconnect, buried in the subground. The display wall was installed for artistic rather than functional effect. Human beings seemed to need some assurance that a hidden supermachine was operating.

Rob and his tutor entered one of the booths. Rob sat down in the bucket in front of the console. He programmed in his name and student ident number. Then he used the keyboard to inform the computer that he was requesting a loan of three thousand microcredits against future earnings.

A rectangular panel set in the curved housing above the keyboard flashed, *State reason.*

Rapidly Rob typed out, *Personal emergency.*

Exfore was busy manipulating a dial in its left side just above its waist. The dial released a small metal plate at the approximate position occupied by the left ribs in a human being. From the opening Exfore pulled a cable with a tiny twelve-prong plug. The robot inserted the cable into a jack on the keyboard housing.

*Number of Robot Tutor who will approve request,* the panel flashed.

"It is not necessary to key in my name," Exfore advised. "I am already connected."

For roughly one minute Exfore stood without moving. Via the cord, he and the Home computer conversed in silence. Rob's palms began to feel chilly. There was a fluttering in his stomach. What if the computer turned him down?

Exfore unplugged. It folded up the cable, stowed it away, and closed the receptacle cover on its metal skin. The interrogation panel above the housing went dark. Somewhere in the subground, bits of information about Rob were being collected: his scholastic record; his extrapolated earnings potential based upon various models of minimum, moderate, and high college success; probable modes of employment following his six years of higher education. Rob guessed that the computer was considering a hundred or more possible futures for him.

The interval seemed long as eternity. Exfore remained unmoving, its photocells dulled. Only the sound of Rob's breathing disturbed the silence.

Finally the panel lighted. Rob almost whooped with joy.

*Request for loan approved. Voucher available at Autobursar 0900 tomorrow.*

The message wiped. It was followed by a new one. *Document of agreement already forwarded to your room for signature. Complete and return via chute.* After another wipe, the mechanical brain added one of those thoroughly impractical touches with which the designers tried to humanize their equipment. The panel printed, *Good luck. That is all.*

Rob was a little astounded by the simplicity. It didn't take much these days to mortgage your future. Of course the quick reply was based on the fact that his record was good, and showed every prospect of remaining so. Exfore, however, raised the touchy subject of exams once again as they went back to the stairwell.

"When you make your travel arrangements in the city,

Rob, be certain that you allow plenty of time for your return trip. A week and a half might not be overdoing it."

"The FTLS operate pretty much on schedule these days," Rob countered.

"Yes, but it is wise to give yourself a margin." As they got off the stairs at the Tutorial Level, Exfore maximized its photocells to stress the message. "If for some reason, however good and sufficient, you should not return by the end of the four-week holiday, your place in the examinations will be taken by another student."

"And I'll get a tenth-rate job, and it'll take me the rest of my life to repay the loan. I'll be here in time, Exfore."

"I certainly hope so."

"Exfore . . ." Rob's throat felt clogged. It was hard to speak. "Thanks again for helping."

"I had no hesitation about recommending approval to the computer. I have faith in you. Founded on a solid base of facts, naturally. I would stop you from going to Stardeep if I could. I know I cannot. You are afflicted with human feelings that are important to you. After the quarter is over, I would welcome the opportunity to wish you bon voyage."

Rob thought about this a moment. "That would be fine. But I don't want to tell anyone else where I'm going."

"None of your friends?"

"I think it's best that way." And would save a lot of humiliation if nothing turned up on Stardeep, Rob added silently.

"Whatever you say."

"Good night, Exfore." Rob turned quickly to the stairs.

The robot tutor remained a moment longer. The beams from its simulated eyes probed down onto the softly clacking treads. Then, with a rustle of relays that sounded almost like a sigh, it glided off in the other direction.

The railcar came out of the tunnel with its running lights blurred to purple streaks. The time was well along toward dawn. Rob had chosen this car because those few students leaving for the four-week holiday probably wouldn't be pulling out till morning.

He was right. He and Exfore were the only ones on the platform. The railcar door glided up on silver shafts. Rob picked up his bubblegrip. He felt cold, very much alone. In the grip were his few items of clothing, his passage cards, the fax of his father, and the diary. He hadn't looked at the diary in months. He meant to do it on the trip.

In total, the contents of his grip seemed very little for a journey across half a galaxy.

The purple running lights changed to red. Rob jumped aboard. "Stay oiled, Exfore."

The robot adjusted its plates into a smile. "Safe journeying, Rob. Come back in four weeks."

"In four weeks," Rob called as the railcar door closed and sealed.

Four weeks. The time seemed so short. But he could feel good about one thing. He'd done well in the end-of-quarter tests.

The railcar picked up speed. Exfore dwindled to a blur of polished metal and photocell light. Rob settled into a pneumolounge. He was the car's only occupant.

The railcar shot into the transparent part of the double tunnel. On the level above ran the autoroads for individual vehicles. A heavy service train of footpads could be seen up there, moving in the direction of the Home. Its headbeams were bright in the darkness.

Soon the service train was gone. The railcar hummed on its single track, traveling just over two hundred toward the stark white-chalk mountain. Dellkart IV looked frozen and unfriendly in the pale glow of its three small moons.

*Four weeks,* the railcar seemed to hum. *Only four weeks, four weeks.* The car plunged into the double mountain tunnel.

Before long Rob glimpsed lights ahead. That was the city. There he would pick up the shuttle rocket to Margoling, the planet where he would board the FTLS. The railcar blazed toward the lights, carrying him forward to Stardeep and back into the painful past.

# Five

# THE CURIOUS MR. LUMMUS

FTLS *Goldenhold 2* was in its last lightjump and on schedule. The week aboard the gigantic freighter had dragged unmercifully. impatient for planetfall, Rob lay in the sling-bunk in the tiny cabin which was the most luxurious accommodation the cargo ship offered.

There were a handful of passengers aboard in similar quarters. Rob had eaten meals with them at the spartan autocaf. Most of them were businessmen. Three were getting off at Stardeep. The rest would ride *Goldenhold 2* to its final destination, Blaketower, the capital world of the Lens End Nebula systems.

The slingbunk rocked ever so gently from side to side. Beyond the end of the bunk was the cabin's single port. It was really an anachronism. A passenger could see out of it only during the moments prior to blastoff and touchdown. Within seconds after leaving a launchyard, the ports of the vessel automatically opaqued as the computers and the Lightcommander completed the shift into hyperspace.

All during the long, silent realtime trip through that *other* space, the ports shimmered with weird, oily spectrums of visible light. No human being had ever glimpsed the *other* space through which the FTLS traveled. Nor was it space in the conventional sense. Rather, it was a series of convoluted space-time warps that somehow coexisted at the fringes of reality. These could be entered and mapped by bouncewaves, but never looked on by human eyes.

Trying to comprehend what any FTLS did while bridging between points of the real universe via hyperspace, Terrans applied the verb *travel*. Unfortunately this suggested a conventional space vessel operating under conventional nuclear power at near lightspeed between closely spaced, conventional worlds.

When the FTLS entered hyperspace, however, it actually de-molecularized into a near infinity of micro-particles, as though a rock had been shattered so that its pieces could pass through a mesh.

But the mesh of hyperspace was twisted, multidimensional, apparently endless. And when the de-molecularized rock—the ship—passed through the portion of the continuing mesh for an extended time, the particles did not scatter as ordinary rock particles would have done. Powerful fields kept the ship and its passengers coherent, functioning, during the entire trip. Then, at the other end of the mesh, which was traversed at faster-than-light speeds, the ship re-molecularized and emerged, conforming perfectly again to the known laws of a known cosmos.

In astromathematics Rob had studied some of the fundamental equations relating to this mode of travel—the word was almost inescapable—and while he could grasp a little of the theory, it was never so real to him as the metaphor of the rock. He, and the ship, were this moment scattered in a trillion tiny fragments. But the special fields made it seem as though nothing had changed, and he was cruising at sublight speed along familiar star lanes.

Optical laws were different in *other* space too. Eyes simply did not function as eyes, because—theory stated—there were no light sources to produce vision. Still, Rob always wondered what lay outside the ports. Perhaps a few men had seen, if *seen* was not another misleading term. Men who rode ships whose systems or Lightcommanders failed; men who were destroyed somewhere in the awful unknown dimension that great ships leaped across, making parsecspanning journeys. Had Lightcommander Duncan Edison seen that *other* space seven years ago? Rob wondered, staring at the page of the diary he had been reading.

Useless to speculate. He was better off examining the ideas in the diary his father had penned.

In an age of almost totally mechanized communication, diaries remained one of the few personally written documents of the human race. Rob liked to return to the diary from time to time because it helped him to know the Lightcommander as nothing else did. The words on the small ruled pages were inscribed with a deep-blue stylus. They were boldly, forcefully formed.

Rob was rereading an entry dated only six days before the fatal launch of *Majestica*.

*... and I am in awful doubt about what to do about my second.*

The reference was to Edison's second in command, Lightadjutant Thomas Mossrose. The man was little more than a name to Rob. But obviously he had been a man who troubled Lightcommander Edison deeply.

*There is no getting around the fact that Mossrose is one of the very few untalented misfits who manage to get into the Space Service. I sensed this when he was first assigned to the ship a month ago. Now I am sure of it. This is his first line command and he simply isn't qualified for it. Should I file a report? I think not, since that is enough to ruin a man for life, both in the service and out. I really believe that the wisest course—from the human standpoint anyway (I wish I could be "wise" like the Machine in the bowels of this monster, that super-smart, all-knowing, hundred-billion-bit-of-knowledge devil that gives me such an inferiority complex)—is to give Mossrose more responsibility rather than less.*

Rob's eye skipped from the reference to the FTLS computer to the next entry, apparently written the same day. It was headed simply, "Later."

*I thought about it while I ate tonight. I am positive Tom Mossrose is incompetent, especially in astromathematics and intratemporal theory. I am afraid that if he were ever placed in full command of the ship, I would have to be at his shoulder every minute, perhaps plugged into the Machine myself, in a tandem linkup to make certain nothing went wrong. There are too many men on board for me to endanger them for the sake of a single Lightadjutant who somehow got by the Placements.*

*But maybe I can train Mossross. Sharpen him up. Find areas of extra responsibility to train him bit by bit. It's either that or file a report and ask fo a new man. And in every other way except professionally, Tom M. is likable. Warm, friendly, bright. I can't destroy him. At least not on this voyage . . .*

There, in a flurry of asterisks and exclamation marks, the day's entry ended.

The diary itself concluded a page or two later. Lightcommander Edison had been caught up in the final preparations for *Majestica*'s run from Hoggen's Star to Stardeep to Blaketower. The last entry, made on Stardeep, was sad and brief.

*What a forlorn place. Much to do. Trying to bring Mossrose along. Uncertain business, that.* More asterisks. One large exclamation point. The rest of the pages were blank.

Rob closed the little book on his stomach. Its sonolock snapped shut, to be opened again only by repetition of the Lightcommander's full name.

On the ports the oily light was crawling from cyan to magenta. The intercall rang.

"All passengers for Stardeep," said a scratchy voice. "All passengers for Stardeep, your attention, please. Scheduled planetfall is 1100. Please report to the lounge within one hour of preliminary customs and medical registration."

Frowning, Rob uncoiled his lean frame from the bunk. His blue eyes were puzzled. He had known there would be a customs check, of course. But this business about medical registration was something new. He thought he had completed all the necessary Communicable Disease History forms before boarding on Margoling.

Well, might as well get it over with. He slipped on his tan jacket with its ornamental collar of white myx fur and left the cramped cabin.

Two levels down, the businessmen who Rob had met at meals had already shown up for registration. They were gathered at an oval floating table. The freighter's purser, who doubled as Fourth Mate, was distributing styli and multileaved forms.

"Fill out each one, please," the purser was saying as Rob approached. He repeated the message to each man. The businessmen took the forms to various small floating tables scattered around the metal-walled, harshly lighted chamber. Soon just Rob and one other passenger were left.

The man standing between Rob and the purser was an overweight fellow whose dress boots, breeches, and blouse, though of obviously expensive glitterfabric, were stained and spotted by a miscellany of dust, grime, and food specks. The man had a head shaped like a melon.

"Lot of nonsense, these forms," the man said. His voice

sounded as though it was filtered through a container of pebbles.

"Yes, sir, I agree," the purser replied smoothly. "But the Stardeep Conservancy Patrol insists on them."

"All for the sake of those little beggars," the man complained.

The purser hooked up an eyebrow. "Sir?"

"Those little beggars the Empts."

"That's right, ah, Mister—" The purser hesitated, ran his eye down a checklist. All names but two had been marked off with a bright orange stylus. "Mr. Lummus?"

"Barton Lummus." The man growled, as though he were angry about having to answer.

The purser strove for politeness. "Haven't seen much of you this trip, have we, sir? At least I don't remember you at the autocaf any—"

"Prefer to stay by myself." Lummus snatched the forms and a black stylus. He turned, looked startled to see Rob standing behind him.

Lummus had a face as white as a nutrient pudding. A scraggly little beard decorated his chin. Several rolls of fat formed extra chins below that. The brown pupils of his eyes were huge. Rob had the uncomfortable feeling that those eyes were like lenses, recording everything about him.

"Pardon me, young master," Lummus said in his rattling voice. "Step right up. Your turn to become enfolded in the web of bureaucracy. We'll be manhandled by the Conpats before we're through, mark my word. Stardeep is a regular dictatorship, and they're the dictators." Flourishing the forms for extra emphasis, Lummus moved off to one of the floating tables.

The purser watched him go, smiled. "Odd chap." He consulted his list. "You're the last, so you're Edison, correct? Here."

"What's this medical registration all about?" Rob asked.

"Actually it's pretty much of a duplication. You probably filed most of the pertinent information before departure. But the Empts are extremely susceptible—"

"Who or what are the Empts?"

"The little beasties native to Stardeep. Never heard of them?"

Rob shook his head.

The purser drew on a tablet with his stylus. First he sketched a circle.

"Basically they're gelatinous. Ball-shaped. They're covered with a kind of armor plate—"

The stylus shaded in the plates.

"Two big eyes."

He drew them, with many facets.

"They lay eggs, and they travel by extending pseudopods of their inner bodies. They have a peculiar cry, too."

The purser uttered a squeak that sounded something like *chee-wee, chee-wee.* From the floating table where he was laboring over his forms, Barton Lummus threw a scowl. A couple of the other businessmen frowned.

"The medical exam isn't all that bad," the purser went on to explain. "You'll be sprayed with special germicides and given an ultrabroad antibio injection just in case you're carrying any viral infection. Takes about five minutes. And it helps protect the Empts. Our friend over there made a mountain out of nothing. Just turn the forms in when we make planetfall." The purser picked up his list, touched his braided cap, and moved off.

Carrying the forms, Rob looked around for a place to write. Unfortunately his choice was limited to the purser's station or one of the smaller tables right next to the one at which the fat man sat. The man was chewing moodily on the end of his stylus. There was something about him that Rob didn't like.

He went to the small table anyway, dialed the pneumo-stool to a comfortable height, sat down.

The back of his neck began to itch. He was being watched.

He concentrated on the forms. Abruptly a voice said, "Ridiculous, what?"

Rob glanced up. Those lenslike brown eyes regarded him with intense curiosity.

"Oh, they don't seem so bad," he said.

"Wait till you run afoul of one of those Conpats. Most of them are young and tough. They're in complete control of the planet, don't you see? They swagger around to show you they know it."

In spite of himself, Rob was interested. "Who are the Conpats? Policemen?"

"Not exactly. They guard the Empt reservations."

"Oh, yes. The purser told me about the Empts."

"Valuable little beggars," Lummus said in a more confidential tone. He waved his stylus flamboyantly. "Did you know that almost the entire planet of Stardeep is their private preserve?"

"No, I didn't know that. I've never been to Stardeep before."

Lummus stroked his scraggly beard. "Neither have I."

"But you know all about the Empts." Somehow Rob felt like laughing.

Laughter was the wrong reaction. Lummus leaned forward in a vaguely threatening way. "It's my business to know a lot of things about a lot of planets, young master. I'm a travel agent. Twice a year I visit various worlds in search of new sights, thrills, and experiences to recommend to my jaded clientele. Bunch of rich riffraff, I'll have you know. But they pay the credits—yes they do. I decided to include Stardeep in my itinerary this trip. Never seen it before. Now I'm wondering if I want to."

To this Rob had no immediate reply. He supposed it was logical for Lummus to brief himself ahead of time on the characteristics of a world he was planning to explore. But it struck Rob as strange that Lummus had already formed such definite and hostile opinions about the Conservancy Patrolmen, who apparently looked after the welfare of some rather helpless-sounding extra-terrestrial Empts. He kept all this to himself, however, because Mr. Lummus seemed angry at everything and everyone. At this very moment he was darting sharp glances toward the men at the other floating tables.

Rob completed the customs information form and tucked it beneath the medical blanks he had already filled out. Uncomfortably, he realized that Barton Lummus was peering at him again.

"Never been to Stardeep, you say? Then what brings you?"

"Family business." Robb stood up, anxious to get away. "My father's estate—"

He muttered the last words while turning to go. He hoped they would satisfy the inquisitive travel agent. They did just the opposite.

"Estate, young master? Settling for a tidy sum of money, are you?" Lummus' eyes shone.

"No, no, just a small piece of property, that's all." Rob strode away so abruptly that Lummus registered complete surprise. Lummus couldn't resist a parting shot.

"If your property is worth anything, the Conpats will

haul you into court and have it devalued. Yes, they will! They'll seize it for part of the infernal reservation. Police-men—bureaucracy—officials—you can't trust any—"

The clang of the sliding hatch cut off the rest of the dia-tribe.

Barton Lummus certainly had an active dislike of all au-thority, Rob thought. But something Lummus had said piqued Rob's interest, and he forgot the stranger, wonder-ing instead about the creatures called the Empts.

There were no references to them in his father's diary. Various planets he had studied in courses at the two Homes were inhabited by equally strange life forms, some quite large. But Rob had never before heard about any kind of extra-terrestrial life that Terran men would label valuable. He wondered about the reason for it.

He would soon find out. Planetfall was still scheduled for 1100 tomorrow.

At table that night—with Lummus nowhere to be seen—Rob tried hard to join the conversation of his fellow passengers. The boring week of lightjumping was coming to an end, and everyone else was in a cheerful mood.

One of the men who was getting off at Stardeep, a tech-nosalesman of giant nuclear-powered pumps, was an excel-lent storyteller. He reeled out anecdote after anecdote about his experiences on this or that out-of-the-way planet. Everybody laughed except Rob.

Later, in his slingbunk, he wondered why. He under-stood quickly enough.

A week of his four was already spent. And he was only now arriving at the place where he might be able to clear the blot from his father's record.

But what if he couldn't?

Rob slept poorly that night.


Next morning, to the accompaniment of ringing bells, the port in his little cabin lost its opacity. He looked out while FTLS *Goldenhold 2* thundered down stern first through the thin cloud layer.

Suddenly the clouds broke. A windy wasteland stretched toward purplish mountain crags. Near at hand Rob glimpsed geodesics glimmering in the light of a pale lemon sun. The city where they were landing seemed to be set down in the middle of the waste, with no roads leading away from it in any direction.

The light-freighter dropped lower. The skeletal black outlines of launchyard cranes appeared against the sky. Then the thrusters of the FTLS cut off in a boil of gray smoke. The stern dropped neatly into its great circular bed. Immense padded rings closed, locking the ship in upright position.

Stardeep. Rob picked up his bubblegrip and rushed into the corridor.

Someone collided with him, stumbled back with an exclamation. Rob started to apologize. A hand clasped his shoulder suddenly.

Despite its layers of fat, the hand of Barton Lummus was strong. It dug into Rob's shoulder until he felt a twinge of pain. Lummus' huge brown eyes shone in the dim corridor.

"Be careful, young master!" Lummus shouted.

Rob apologized somewhat angrily. Lummus let go of his shoulder. He got control of himself, flicked several specks off his coat of glitterfabric. Then he hurried on, lugging a large, floridly decorated bubblegrip.

The man's outburst left Rob shaken. It was all out of proportion to the offense. He wondered whether Barton Lummus was really a travel agent or something else.

Rob shook his head, waited a minute, then moved down the same corridor Lummus had taken to reach the unloading pod.

# Six

## OF EMPTS AND GREEN JUICE

Travel agent Lummus had barged to the head of the line at the automated customs station. Rob was separated from him by the other businessmen leaving the ship. Rob felt relieved.

From a position near the oval door leading out of the customs room a young, sunburned man with quick eyes and a cool manner surveyed each one of the arrivals. He wore a trim black uniform and high boots. Small gold emblems decorated his shoulders. The man didn't carry any kind of sidearm, but he had an air of tough authority that suggested he wouldn't need one.

A Conservancy Patrolman? Lummus practically confirmed it. He collected his luggage as it popped out of the maw of the radiograph, then glared at the young man in black—while the latter's head was turned.

Lummus rushed out.

Rob slipped his bubblegrip onto the moving belt. The belt carried it under the first inspection scope. A short taped message was repeated over the loudspeakers, courtesy of the local Commercial Association:

"Welcome to the planet Stardeep and the city of Churchill, capital of the North Continent. The atmosphere of our planet is breathable, Terran-4 class. Mask suits are not required. The population of Churchill, largest city on the planet, is 40,000. You will find all types of commercial establishments at your disposal. May we suggest that if your activities will take you outside the city, you check either with the Spacefarer's Aid booth in the lobby or with the headquarters of the Conservancy Patrol. Special permits

42

are required for travel in certain areas of the countryside. When you are finished with customs, kindly leave by the doorway marked with the large green M. You will be processed through medical in the shortest possible time. Thank you for your attention."

When Rob's grip reappeared at the end of the belt, he took it through the indicated doorway. He found himself in a long covered passageway connecting one geodesic dome with another. The walls of the passage filtered out the heaviest rays of the lemon-hued sun while presenting a clear panorama of the surroundings.

Through the right wall Rob saw the domes of Churchill. Aircar ways threaded through the city above the walkways, which were at ground level. To the left, a busy FTLS launchyard stretched out to where the waste began.

By craning his neck, Rob could see back to the *Goldenhold 2*, a huge, sleek cylinder jutting to the sky. Hundreds of men swarmed around the lip of the concrete pit into which the ship had settled. Other, smaller commercial craft were also docked in the yard. With a stinging feeling Rob realized that this was probably the last sight Lightcommander Edison had seen before *Majestica*'s ports opaqued and she went five milliseconds into hyperspace and—*what?*

Illuminated arrows directed him to a small, blue-tiled room where another taped voice instructed him to strip and place his bubblegrip and clothing in a hopper. The hopper promptly flopped back into the wall and sealed itself shut.

Valves in the ceiling opened, bathing Rob in a pleasantly-scented antiseptic mist. A second, colder mist replaced the first. It left him feeling almost unbearably clean. The hopper popped open. His clothes were returned.

They felt warm, smelled freshly laundered. Sonics, probably. He was just tugging on his tunic when a middle-aged tech with a penedermic in one hand walked in.

The barrel of the injecting device was already marked with a piece of tape machine-punched with Rob's name. Medical precautions on Stardeep were certainly efficient.

"This is just a broad-spec antibio," the tech began. "You probably heard about it on board ship."

Rob nodded. "So I don't spread germs to the Empts."

"Correct. Sleeve back, please."

Rob rolled up his cuff. The tech placed the fan-shaped muzzle of the penedermic against his arm just above his elbow. There was a quick sensation of dozens of tiny needles pricking his skin. The wall opened. The tech tossed the penedermic into a chute that sucked it away.

He spread his hands, grinned. "That's it. You're excused."

Rob rolled his cuff down again. "Why so many precautions?"

"Have you heard much about our little friends the Empts?"

"Some. They're armored, oviparous, travel via their pseudopods. And they're valuable. No one's told me why, though."

The tech leaned against the door. "Not because of their intelligence, certainly. That's rudimentary. But get close to one and you'll find out soon enough."

Interested, Rob asked, "What happens if I get close?"

"No one's really succeeded in explaining it yet, but the Empts radiate some kind of mental energy. At close range it exerts a definite psychochemical change in a human being. You forget everything and anything unpleasant in the past. And I mean everything. Psychomedics all over the galaxy use live Empts to treat mentally disturbed patients. The psychomeds call the process Empting, partly because of the Empts themselves, and partly because the treatment literally empties the patient's mind of all his traumatic memories."

"So that's the reason these Conservancy Patrolmen protect them."

A nod from the tech. "Right. All told, the Empt population is small. A very few are allotted to the general population as pets. Maybe a dozen a year. The rest are guarded out on the reservations. Left alone until special hunting teams go in, pick out a few, and ship them to various medical centers around the planets."

Ready to leave, Rob said. "Thanks for the explanation. I can see why they're so valuable. I could use a little Empting once in a while myself."

"Couldn't we all?" the tech grinned and waved farewell.

As Rob swung along toward the lobby of the huge port dome, he thought about the curious little creatures who inhabited the planet. For a minute he wished that he had one of his own. How much easier it would be simply to forget *Majestica*, return to Dellkart IV, and never again be troubled by memories of the past.

Unfortunately it wouldn't work that way. He had to find the answers if he could. His step quickened. Just being on Stardeep after a journey that would have taken thirty-two realtime years in a conventional starship gave him a new sense of confidence.

He located the lobby kiosk with the illuminated sign reading SPACEFARER'S AID. He stepped around to the rear and came upon a robot seated at a rather battered desk.

The robot was a much cheaper model than Exfore, and it had definitely seen better days. Its neck joints had corroded, giving an odd cock to its head. One of its photocells kept blinking on and off.

"Hel-lo," said the robot. "May Spacefarer's Aid be of service, service, service, ser—*rrawk!*"

The robot made a fist and banged its own head. Then it finished, "—service?"

"There's a Phylex Monitor Station about a hundred miles from here. Is that in a restricted area?"

"But definitely," the robot replied. "The station is located behind the electronic barrier." The contraption—Rob couldn't think of it as a person, the way he sometimes thought of Exfore—uttered a series of peculiar metallic coughs. Something noisy took place in its innards, as though a bucket of bolts had been upset. "But definitely. The station is located behind—*rrawk!*"

The robot hit its head again. Things seemed to straighten out.

"Everything behind the electronic barrier is off limits?" Rob wanted to know.

"But absolutely. Only the Conpats are allowed past. You might get special permission."

"How would I go about that?"

"Go to Conpat Headquarters on Avenue Ursus. Speak to the Commander, Simon Ling."

"Ling. Thanks very much."

"Don't mention—*rrawk!*—but definitely—*rrawk!*—but absolutely—" The blinking photocell began to exude a trickle of smoke. The robot's tone sounded almost pitiful. "Service, please. Please call the service department before—*rrawk! rrawk! rrawk!*"

This time the robot clanged its head with both fists, to no avail. It kept emitting raucous cries as Rob raced to the main administration desk on the other side of the lobby

and punched in a picphone request. He relayed the plea for
service to yet another robot.

By the time he left the building, three shiny repair robots
were converging on the kiosk, from which smoke was now
belching in quantity.

Rob stepped into the sunlight. The thinner atmosphere
cut sharply into his lungs, making him gasp for breath.

Walking slowly, he headed down the broad rampway of
the spaceport building. In a few moments his system adjusted to the fresh air. He had been breathing processed ox-
ygen inside the FTLS for so many days that he had
forgotten how a true atmosphere smelled.

There were traces of mint and cinnamon in the air of
Stardeep, and a dusty tang too. Between geodesics he
caught glimpses of the forlorn desert stretching away
toward the purple mountains. A brisk, warm wind blew
steadily from that direction.

Churchill seemed a pleasant, if not overly modern, town.
There were mothers with children on the streets, the usual
quota of clerical and service workers, men in coveralls
from the FTLS launchyard, and an occasional Conpat
walking briskly on some errand. Rob saw nothing resem-
bling an Empt, however.

Overhead, vehicular traffic whizzed on the aircar ways.
The ways cut off the direct sunlight and made the walkways below pleasant and comfortable. Since it was nearly
noon Galactic Mean Time, Rob decided to find a place to
stay and then have lunch before calling on Simon Ling at
Conpat Headquarters.

He came to a broad pedestrian boulevard, which he discovered was the Avenue Ursus. He proceeded along it for a
block or two, finding a small, comfortable hostel just
around one corner. He deposited his bubblegrip in his room
and then went out to a central caf, which he had noticed
on Avenue Ursus.

The moving belt carried him from the entrance to the
head of one of the selection lines. As a tray popped from a
chute, Rob noticed an attractive girl just in front of him.
She was his own age, or perhaps a year younger. Long
straw-colored hair hung down between her shoulders,
caught into a tail with a ring of brass. He could only see
her face in profile, but it seemed quite pretty, dominated by
eyes of a much brighter blue than Rob's own. The girl wore
a white single-piece resort outfit. The handle of a shopall

was looped over one wrist. In the shopall were several small parcels.

The belt carried cafeteria customers up the line past holograms of the various items offered for sale. With a start Rob realized that the girl and her companion, a shorter, heavier girl, had been busy selecting their food while he had been busy gawking. He had already passed the soups and other appetizers and was just coming up on the nutrient drinks.

Quickly he stepped onto one of the little stationary platforms alongside the belt. He fished in his pocket for a unicredit, slipped the small disc into the slot under a tempting holographic image of a large goblet of bright green vitalime. The door lid flew open. He fitted the goblet stem into the appropriate recess on his tray. Then he stepped back onto the moving platform.

Just ahead in the entree section, the straw-haired girl and her friend were returning to the belt with their selections. At the same time, a worker from the launchyard was trying to get past them to go back to the soups. A wheeled robot hostess buzzed its buzzer at him and demanded that he leave the belt, walk to the beginning, and come through again the regular way.

But the worker was in a hurry. As the belt carried Rob on, the worker squeezed past the two girls and headed his way.

Rob knew it was either step off or get bowled aside. He had one foot on the entree platform, one on the moving belt, and his tray balanced in both hands. The worker rushed past, hitting his elbow. Rob let out an exclamation. The moving belt jerked his left foot, threw him off balance. His tray tipped. The goblet of vitalime fountained out its contents—

Straight onto the back of the pretty girl's resort costume.

The girl's stout companion let out an *"Ooooo!"* Rob watched horrified as the electric green stain spread through the fibers of the girl's white outfit.

The girl spun. Rob caught the blaze of her blue eyes full force. "It feels like I'm an absolute mess, you—you *space-clod!*"

The stocky girl giggled. "Don't lose your temper, Lyn. But I guess you already have."

"I'm sorry," Rob said. "That man—"

He gaped. Somehow, the hurrying worker had disappeared.

At the beginning belt, the other customers were complaining and urging Rob to get moving. The girl tried to look over her shoulder at the hideous green stain.

"And I just bought this outfit this morning. I should think you could at least say you're sorry!"

Rob's temper heated. "I already did! Look, it really was an accident—"

"Typical offworlder excuse!" the girl cried. She had noted his Dellkart IV clothing.

"Won't you even listen to an apology?"

"When I paid my whole allowance for this—this ruined rag?"

"Now Rob's cheeks were red. "O.K., O.K.,! I'll pay for sonic cleaning!"

The girl's blue eyes crackled. "You certainly will!"

His own anger stoked by hers, Rob snapped. "Where shall I send the money?"

"To me, of course. My name is—" Her friend was tugging at her arm. "What, Beth?"

"Better not give him your home code if he just got off a ship." The stocky girl's melodramatic eye-rollings indicated she suspected the worst of interplanetary travelers.

The pretty girl evidently thought Beth's idea made sense, though. In a quieter but no less firm voice, she said, "You can reach me in care of Conpat Headquarters. My father is the Commander. Just leave the credit voucher for Lyndsey Ling."

Turning, she was carried away up the belt with her friend.

"Belt it or get off, space bum," someone yelled from the caf entrance.

Rob got off.

He stood on the entree platform, looking dismayed. The last of the green vitalime dribbled off the tray he held slack at his side. He stared at the straw-colored hair vanishing down around a bend in the belt. He said, half aloud:

"Her father's the Commander?"

Just how far would he get now with his request to enter the Empt reservation?

# Seven

## CONPAT COMMANDER

Simon Ling tented his fingers, leaned back in the gray chair hovering just off the floor, and said, "That's a fascinating story, young man. And a most unusual request, I might add. Not exactly in line with Conservancy Patrol policy. You'll have to give me a moment to think about it."

There was nothing else for Rob to say. He sat on the opposite side of a large natural wood desk in the Commander's comfortable office. The office was located on an upper floor of the Headquarters geodesic on Avenue Ursus. It was a cool, shady room, made more friendly by the warm highlights of the hardwood—a rarity in these days of plasto and alloy.

Several sections of the outer wall were transparent sheets of solarscreen, affording a glareless view of the town. Around the office were a number of momentos of Simon Ling's career: a framed scroll of commendation; a Conpat Academy degree; a swagger stick in a glass case; a large color litho showing a small, round, armoured creature with faceted eyes.

An Empt, very likely. The little extra-terrestrial looked almost comical, except for its eyes. They seemed a little sad.

Rob fidgeted. Ling inscribed another note on the tablet where he had written a few comments as Rob explained his reasons for coming to Stardeep. The Commander stood up, scratched the back of his neck as he stared thoughtfully toward a distant crag.

Simon Ling was a massive, big-boned man. He stood nearly six and a half feet tall. Like the Conpat that Rob had seen at the spaceport, he was deeply tanned. He had brown eyes and pleasant, if irregular, features highlighted by a bold hooked nose. His hair showed streaks of white, though Rob guessed him to be only about forty. He wore the black Conpat uniform and high black boots. But the gold emblems on his shoulders—intertwined letters, C and P—were inlaid with tiny rubies.

At length the Commander said, "The Phylex Monitor Stations are the joint property of the space lines. Strictly off limits."

"That I understand," Rob nodded. "But I was hoping for special permission—"

He halted in midsentence. Ling studied him. Rob had the uncomfortable feeling that the girl named Lyndsey had already communicated with her father. He was beaten before he started. And all because of a clumsy mistake.

Simon Ling sat down again. He tossed one boot up to rest on the desk corner. "On the other hand, you've come a very long way through hyperspace. At your own expense, I gather."

"Yes, sir."

"And your time on Stardeep is strictly limited."

Thinking of the oppressive deadline, Rob nodded. "I'm holding a return passage on *Goldenhold 2* when she comes back through."

Ling toyed with the sheet of notes. "Do you really think you'll learn anything by interrogating the tapes at the station? I wasn't serving here when the agents of the Inquiry Commission looked into the *Majestica* matter. But I understand they stayed in Churchill for over a month and visited that station nearly every day. They went over and over those tapes."

Rob felt the old futility. Some of his tension showed through as he replied, "Probably I won't find too much, Commander. But I have to try. I have to hear those tapes for myself."

Simon smiled. "Well, I admire your motives and your persistence. I hope you won't be disappointed."

Rob's stomach flipflopped. Did that last remark mean that the Commander was going to grant permission for the visit? Maybe he was living with luck on his side after all!

Perhaps the Commander's daughter hadn't shown up yet. Rob decided he had done the wise thing by rushing directly to Headquarters as soon as he finished his meal at the central caf.

Simon Ling reached into his desk, pulled out a musicpipe. He touched the controls and stuck the pipestem in his mouth. Smoke, fragrant and sweet, puffed from the bowl. The strains of a very old symphony drifted from the tiny speaker.

"You do know," Ling resumed, "that the Phylex Station is one hundred and ten miles out in the waste."

"Yes, sir. But I presume there's a way to reach it."

"The only way is in a programmed Conpat flyer. There won't be one available for a couple of days. I keep my men busy. We have nearly a whole continent to cover, and right at this time of year we're thinning the Empt population. Twice annually we gather up several dozen for shipment to various hospitals and medical installations. This is one of those times."

Again Rob didn't know what to say. The Commander seemed to be encouraging and discouraging him at the same time.

Simon Ling puffed twice on his musicpipe. With each puff the symphony grew louder for a moment. He drew a punch form out of his desk. As he poised his stylus above it, something else apparently occurred to him.

"We wouldn't be able to provide you with a Conpat escort."

"But I don't know how to run a flyer, sir."

"Perhaps you didn't hear me a moment ago. Our flyers are programmed. If I give you permission to make the trip, we'll prepare an electronically coded card. All you do is place the card in the flyer's control slot. The card will activate the flyer onto the right course across the waste. There won't be anyone else aboard. The card will land the flyer and also program it to take off after a specified interval. Two hours, probably. You'll have to be aboard. This is a large continent. I have only two hundred men to cover it. We can't afford to send out extra search parties at thinning time."

"I understand, sir," Rob agreed. "I'll follow orders."

"Ordinarily," Ling continued, "I'd refuse a request for a trip into the reservation right at this time." He waved his pipe toward the faraway crags. "The Empts lay and hatch their young in the caves up in those mountains. At laying time the female Empt can have her hormonal balance thrown off by contact with human beings. As a result, next year's baby Empt population is smaller. When I send my men out to check the waste, they seldom even land their flyers. I don't expect you'll encounter many female Empts at the Phylex Station. But I do want you to appreciate that I have to bend a few rules to let you go."

"It's very kind of you," Rob said.

Now Simon Ling had his stylus ready again. Abruptly, his rather stiff official manner melted, replaced by one of the warmest smiles Rob had ever seen.

"If it were my father, Rob, I'd do the same thing. Now let's see about getting your card made up."

At the instant Commander Ling started to write, Rob heard a noise behind him.

"Hello, Dad. I'm all finished with—*oh*."

Simon Ling laid his stylus aside. Rob stood up. He found himself looking into bright eyes that were full of anger.

"In case you've left the voucher already," Lyndsey Ling said, "you'd better take it back and double it. I stopped at the cleanmat and there's going to be an extra charge for reweaving. That green goo not only leaves big stains, it destroys fibers too."

"I hadn't made arrangements yet—" Rob began.

"Well, you'd better," Lyndsey repeated. "I only bought this outfit this morning."

Suddenly Rob forgot about the danger of angering Commander Ling. The girl's manner struck him as altogether unreasonable. He responded in kind: "Miss Ling, I offered to apologize. You wouldn't accept it. Next I offered to pay the bill and you weren't satisfied with that either. What would you like me to do, synthesize a new outfit by hand?"

In a heavy tone, Simon Ling said, "What in the name of the Empts is going on?"

"This *offworlder*—" Lyndsey cried.

"Your daughter—" Rob said simultaneously.

"One at a time, one at a time!"

Tense silence, then. Rob cast a glum glance at the punch form, untouched, on Ling's desk. The Commander laid his musicpipe aside. A desk receptacle sucked out the glowing coals and ash and the symphony stopped in mid-beat.

Lyndsey flung her shopall down. She turned to show her father the ruined back of her outfit. Rob cringed at the damage. The vitalime had indeed rotted a hole in the white fibers. Their ends looked like charred wires.

"I was in the central caf with Beth," Lyndsey explained, "when this offworlder—"

"Don't use that slang term in my presence," Simon interrupted. "His name is Rob Edison. He's a visitor to Stardeep. Treat him that way."

"But, Dad—!"

"Young lady, I won't warn you again. Mind your manners. Now. I gather this young man spilled something on your blouse?"

Lyndsey glared. "Green, horrible gunk."

"Did he offer to pay to repair the damage?"

"Well, yes. But he's obviously just a bad-mannered space tramp spending his vacation bumming from planet to—"

"Enough!" roared Simon Ling.

The girl huffed, threw another withering glare at Rob, flounced over to a chair, and plumped down in it. The Commander rounded a corner of the desk. Gently he took his daughter's chin in his big fingers, lifted her head.

"I dearly loved your mother, my girl. Finest woman ever born under the Arco stars. But she had a streak of temper I'm afraid you've inherited. Mr. Edison is not a space tramp. He's a student from the Dellkart IV Space League Home at the other end of the galaxy. He's spending what little holiday time he has on a very serious quest. Believe me, his coming to Stardeep isn't frivolous. I think you owe him an apology, rather than the reverse."

For a long moment father and daughter gazed at each other. Then the color in Lyndsey Ling's cheeks heightened. Rob really had to admit she was one of the prettiest girls he had ever met.

At last Lyndsey smacked the toe of her sandal against the floor. "It's just that I saved all my allowance to buy this outfit—"

"And Mr. Edison has offered to undo the damage," Simon reminded her.

"If you've got a blank voucher," Rob said, "I'll sign it with my ident number. Then you can fill in any moment."

Simon shook his head. "Let me take care of it. I know you're willing, but I expect I can afford it better than you, Lyndsey—"

The girl glanced at Rob. She started to smile, but didn't. "Sorry." She looked away.

"My apologies again, too," Rob told her.

Simon chuckled, went back to his desk and picked up the punch form.

"I'll take care of getting this processed, Rob. Just give me your signature."

Rob signed quickly, conscious of the girl watching him. He was relieved when Simon Ling told him that he could simply drop back to Headquarters in the morning and pick up the card.

"I hope we'll have a flyer for you in a day or so," the Commander concluded.

"Thank you very much, sir," Rob said, heading out in a hurry.

Lyndsey stood up, embarrassed. "I didn't mean to call you a space bum."

"Forget it," he said. He meant it. He was glad to be out of a potentially explosive situation.

Rob hummed all the way down the old-fashioned fixed-position staircase to the dome's lobby. Apparently Commander Ling was a widower who understood the whimsicalities of the female mind. Rob's only regret was that he and Lyndsey Ling had started off so badly. In other circumstances, he would like to have gotten to know her. But he hadn't come to Stardeep to find a girl.

As Rob hurried down the front steps leading from the Headquarters dome to the shaded walkways of Avenue Ursus, he noticed a familiar face across the way. Under a yellow-leafed hydrotree, the travel agent, Barton Lummus, sat on a bench.

Next to him sat a male android of Vegan manufacture. The android had emerald-colored hide, completely hairless, and large gray eyes without pupils. As a concession to civilization it wore a pair of neutral-colored shorts. Its face had been formed into a rigid expression that it could never change. But even though the android's mouth was an inflexible slit across its face, it had a vaguely sinister appearance.

Barton Lummus, seedy as ever, was conversing with the artificial human. Rob wondered how a travel agent could afford to rent one of the constructs.

Rob turned onto a walkway. From a corner of an eye he caught a flicker of emotion.

He was disturbed to see that Barton Lummus was watching him. Lummus made no sign of recognition, merely stared hard with those lenslike brown eyes, before returning to conversation with the android.

In the excitement of thinking about his forthcoming trip

to the Phylex Station, Rob soon forgot about the incident altogether.

Next morning, as instructed, Rob turned up at the Headquarters Building on Avenue Ursus.

Commander Simon Ling wasn't in his office. But his robot secretary had the small, embossed plastic card prepared and delivered it into Rob's hands.

He could make no sense of the jumble of electronic characters raised from the gray surface. But he clutched the card like a talisman anyway, slipping it carefully into the inside pocket of his jacket.

"The Commander also left this for you," the secretary said. She passed Rob a note marked PERSONAL.

On his way out of the dome he unfolded the note. It was written in a strong, slanting hand that reminded him of his father's.

> *Dear Rob Edison—My daughter and I talked it over and decided that as citizens of Stardeep, we owe you a somewhat better reception than you received at the central caf. Why don't we make up for that by having a meal together tomorrow? Let's meet for breakfast at the caf, around 0800. Send a message if this won't work out. Otherwise we'll see you then. The meal's on me. Cordially, S. Ling.*

Rob was finishing the note, a grin on his face, as he reached the bottom of the steps outside the dome. Suddenly a heavy weight crashed against his side, spinning him around. The note flew out of his hand and sailed away in the breeze.

"Watch where you're—ah! Young master!"

Righting himself, Rob tried to conceal his surprise. There, flicking specks from his blouse, stood Barton Lummus with his android close at hand.

Lummus patted his pockets as though searching for something. "We seem to have a bent for collision, young master," he said in his pebbly voice. "Like atomic particles, what?"

"This time I don't think it was my fault."

"Even though you had your nose buried in some document which has now blown away?"

"All right, my apologies," Rob growled.

Lummus continued to poke and probe at his pockets. Finally he stopped. His white face pulled downward. "You really should be more careful. You could do serious injury to your elders."

Lummus' several chins quivered. His straggly chin beard danced as he emphasized his words with repeated nods. The emerald android remained just a few paces away, the unnerving, empty gray eyes trained in Rob's direction.

Lummus made a great show of rearranging his soiled blouse into the proper folds. For some puzzling reason, he seemed to grow angrier by the moment. Finally, scowling, he marched over to his android and tugged its arm.

"Come, Blecho, let's move on. Young hotheads make the streets unsafe these days. Someone ought to teach the little beggars some manners." And away he clumped, the perfect picture of injury.

The android swung its head to give Rob another eyeless stare that made him shiver. The two vanished in the crowds along Avenue Ursus. Rob asked himself whether travel agent Lummus was completely right in the head. Did he need a little Empting therapy, perhaps?

That night, in his room at the hostel, Rob discovered something equally odd.

He was piling his clothing on the bed for overnight cleaning in the central sonichute. He had removed all his personal effects and placed them on the small stand. As he folded his shorts, he happened to glance at the gray electronic card.

There was a large, greasy smear on one corner.

He picked up the card, tilted it. Viewed from a right angle, the glistening smear revealed itself to be the print of a human finger.

Suddenly he recalled Lummus blundering into him. Had the man tried to pick his pocket? Perhaps that would explain Lummus' anger. He had failed to net any loot in the encounter. Rob still had all his valuables.

With that android companion, Blecho, Lummus was certainly something besides what he pretended to be.

A petty criminal working the star lanes, maybe? Traveling from planet to planet filching credit cases and jewelry where he could?

Rob tossed his shorts on the pile and shook his head, hoping that he would have no further meetings with that peculiar stranger.

# Eight

## RUNAWAY EMPT

The breakfast at the central caf next morning was an unqualified success.

Encouraged by Simon Ling, Rob ate a whopping meal. He started with a big goblet of nutriorange. Then he downed a quarter rasher of inhumanly expensive real bacon, plus a small copper pot of a salty delicacy called yoyo eggs. These were imported from a nearby planet, the Commander said, and were a favorite among citizens of the Lens End Nebula. On top of all this, two steaming mugs of morning broth spiced with chicory and lively conversation made it an occasion to remember.

Lyndsey Ling looked even prettier, Rob thought, now that she had her temper under control. Her face was animated. Her blue eyes shone with friendly highlights. She had put her straw-colored hair up in a bun and fastened it with amber-headed pins. The aquamarine one-piece that she wore complemented her coloring.

The girl made no mention of the incident with the green juice. Instead, she asked a great many questions about Rob's life on Dellkart IV and customs on the planets in his part of the galaxy. Nothing was said about *Majestica*. No doubt Simon Ling had coached her to avoid the subject.

The Commander let his daughter do most of the talking. He sat back puffing his musicpipe as it played a Mellofors electronic cantata, and he smiled frequently. Well, even if Lyndsey Ling was being nice on orders, Rob enjoyed it. The meal made Stardeep, and his purpose for coming, seem less grim.

Finally, as the tabletop revolved the magno-bottomed

dishes out of sight, Commander Ling finished his pipeful and said, "You did get your card, didn't you, Rob?"

He patted his jacket. "Right here, sir."

"Good. I checked our rosters. Two of my men should be in at sundown. That means a flyer will be available in the morning. Well, I must get back to Headquarters. Do you have plans?"

"Just a little sight-seeing, I suppose," Rob replied. "I want to hear the Phylex tapes before I start asking questions at the launchyard."

Simon nodded. "Lyndsey, if you're not busy, why don't you show Rob around?"

"I half promised Beth—" Lyndsey noticed her father's direct stare. "I'd love to."

They left the central caf. Simon accepted Rob's thanks for the meal and headed up Avenue Ursus toward the Conpat dome. Rob waited until the Commander was out of earshot before saying, "I appreciate the hospitality, Lyndsey. But there's no need for me to tie you up all morning."

"Don't be silly. Beth is probably busy anyway."

On the edge of exasperation, Rob said, "My impressions of Stardeep are just fine. Please don't feel obliged to show me the sights because your dad told you to."

Lyndsey flushed. "To make up for yesterday, you mean? I need to. I was wretched. I'm sorry."

"Let's forget it. Your father tried to smooth things over by taking me to breakfast. I enjoyed it a lot. But—what's wrong?"

Lyndsey looked a trifle embarrassed. "The breakfast was my idea."

"Your—"

"I'm not really a harpy, Rob. True, my mother was fourth-generation colonial Hispanio, and Dad always says I inherited her Latin temper, but I really am sorry for what happened yesterday." Suddenly her eyes crinkled and brightened. "Now we've gotten past all the formal drivel and apologies. I know you're not a space bum, and you know I'm not a complete witch. So shall we go?"

"Deal," he said, laughing as he matched her stride.

They spent an hour in the shopping district, another at the low, quiet dome that housed the Churchill Civic Museum. Although small, the museum had a number of excellent display cases explaining the physiology of the Empts, and a whole room devoted to an operating di-rama that duplicated the city's FTLS launchyard. In this room Rob noticed a bronze plaque hanging in an alcove. A pinspot illuminated the raised lettering. His throat thickened as the words flashed their meaning to his mind:

*IN MEMORIAM, FTLS Majestica.*

He stepped into the alcove and read the plaque. It gave only a few details: the date; the fact that the cause of the tragedy and the fate of the lightship were unknown; the number of officers and crew. His father was shown as Lightcommander.

Lyndsey came up behind him softly. "Dad told me all about why you traveled to Stardeep. I thought you should see it."

She spoke in a soft, intense voice. This was a completely different Lyndsey Ling. The pinspot put reflected lights in her brilliant blue eyes. He realized that she really meant what she was saying. "When I heard the story, well—that's when I became really ashamed of the way I behaved yesterday. You're to be admired for coming to Stardeep, Rob."

Her words warmed him. But something made him say, "Admired? How can that be? Everybody tells me it's a waste of time."

Lyndsey's hair shone as she shook her head. "Admired for loving your father as much as you did. And do."

A relaxed smile spread across his face. "It's nice of you to say that."

Another moment passed. Lyndsey glanced away.

Her tone became more normal as they moved out of the hushed alcove. "If you've seen enough of the museum, how about a more practical visit? Would you like to go see the Conpat flyer yard?"

He said he would. They got aboard walkways that eventually transferred them to the edge of the town.

"There's the yard," Lyndsey said, catching his hand as they stepped off the walkway. In this part of Churchill most of the domes seemed to be devoted to light industry. They crossed a small park built around natural outcroppings of pink-veined rock and approached a compound with a servodome at one side.

A teardrop-shaped craft was parked at a dock built into the dome. The craft was equipped with small fore-and-aft thrusters and ground-effect skids. Two mechs were busy testing the skids with cylinders of compressed gas.

"It looks a lot like the flitters we have on Dellkart IV," Rob told the girl.

He shielded his eyes against the lemon sun. Out past the compound, the air seemed to shimmer. The shimmering effect was continuous into the distance both to the left and the right. It much resembled heat radiation, blurring the waste and the mountains beyond. But Rob knew the weather on Stardeep was too temperate to produce such a condition. Another answer suggested itself.

"Is that one of the electronic barriers?"

Lyndsey replied that it was. "Actually Churchill is right at one limit of the reservation. You can't get past the barrier except in a flyer, and the Conpats have all the flyers. If you tried to get past on foot, you'd be knocked unconscious and your system would be out of whack for a week. It happens now and then. Poachers come here hoping to pick up a few Empts to sell on the gray market. They're never successful, because there is a continuous horizontal barrier too, ten miles up. The reservation is literally inside a protective box."

After taking a closer look at the teardrop flyer with its golden CP enameled into the rigid-resin hull plates, Rob and Lyndsey boarded the walkways back toward the center of town.

They left the ways at Avenue Capricorn, a thoroughfare that ran into Avenue Ursus near the Conpat dome. It was nearing the lunch hour. Shops and stores had disgorged a crowd of people into the shaded streets. Overhead, traffic hummed.

Rob felt good and much less lonely. Up ahead he noticed a dipix palace. Its shining cloud-marquee announced an attraction that had played to a student audience in the Dellkart IV Home auditorium. The galaxy wasn't so huge and forbidding after all—

"I wonder what all the commotion's about," Lyndsey said suddenly.

He followed her pointing finger. The crowds were parting with great haste about a block ahead. Something in furious motion shot past the legs of the men and women who jumped out of the way with great alacrity. Lyndsey and Rob stepped off the walkway onto the mall of brilliant green plasto turf and watched.

The source of the excitement boiled toward them. People were scattering to the walkways on both sides of the mall in near-panic. All at once Rob had a clear view of the cause.

"That's an Empt," he exclaimed.

The small spherical creature was traveling toward them at remarkable speed. It did so by extending three gelatinous pseudopods out between the armored plates of its body, pulling itself ahead and then quickly extending three more pseudopods while the first three retracted. Two large, faceted eyes on the ball-like body caught random beams of sunlight and flashed as the creature sped along. Those eyes were a bright, almost iridescent yellow.

"Someone's pet on the loose," Lyndsey said. "Look at the chain."

A metal ringstaple had somehow been embedded in one of the armor plates on the Empt's dorsal surface. From this hung a short length of clinking alloy chain. The last link was sheared in half.

The Empt was only a square away now and making rapid progress by shooting pseudopods in threes. Rob heard its weird, high-pitched cry—*chee-wee, chee-wee*.

Almost immediately he spotted the Empt's owner. Down the center of the mall a block behind charged a bearded man, waving a wide-brimmed, cone-crowned hat.

"Hold on, critter! Hold on there!"

The man ran with erratic, zigzag steps. As he came closer, Rob saw that his faded blouse and trousers were ripped at the cuffs and incredibly dirty as well. The man's straggly dark hair hung to his shoulders. His beard waved unkempt halfway to his waist. The other end of the broken chain hung from a bracelet on his wrist.

*Chee-wee, chee-wee,* squealed the Empt. It shot straight toward Rob and Lyndsey.

People on the walkways gaped, pointed. Someone shouted for the Conpats. The Empt's blazing yellow eyes mirrored fragments of the scene around it as it came to within twenty feet of Rob, then ten.

Still in frantic pursuit, the bearded man wigwagged his floppy hat and howled for "the critter" to stop.

Without thinking, Rob stepped straight into the Empt's path.

At the same time he heard Lyndsey say, "Not too close, Rob!"

Instinct made him want to help. He dove at the Empt which was now about six feet in front of him. As he launched into his dive, he heard Lyndsey's voice rise higher:

*"Rob—don't!"*

By that time Rob had landed on his stomach and chest. He clamped hands on the faintly moist plates at both sides of the Empt's body. He had a quick, blurred impression of faceted yellow eyes shining like nova stars. There was a mild tingling in his palms. *Chee-wee, chee-wee!*

Then and only then did he really remember the peculiar power of the creatures. By that time, everything around him was sliding, dissolving, collapsing, as though his surroundings were made of the same translucent stuff as the Empt's inner body.

The tingling seemed to reach his brain, muddle his mind. He still had hold of the Empt—his hands told him that much—but all his other senses registered a wild, changing montage of sights and sounds and smells. A portion of the lemon sky of Stardeep melted and slipped to one side. Lyndsey's voice sounded like a whining, overworked motor. Blades of the synthetic turf felt huge as spears against his cheek. *Chee-wee, chee-wee!*

Men shouted for the Conpats. Their voices seemed to echo and ring through windy chasms. The tingling inside Rob's head grew more pronounced. Something faintly slimy touched the back of one of his hands. A thrashing pseudopod? He tried to focus his eyes. He couldn't. The world was revolving like a cartwheel of gelatin.

All at once a face thrust in—a wild, bearded, sun-parched face with eyes like bits of blue grass. The man's mouth was working, spitting words Rob couldn't comprehend. The mouth wrenched to reveal white teeth in startling contrast to the dark cheeks above the untidy beard. The man's blue eyes were both frightened and full of another emotion that might be anger, even hate—

Suddenly there was no longer weight against Rob's palms. He rolled over on his back, gasped for air. Many voices sounded noisily about him. They all resembled overloaded motors. Faces, distorted as though seen in flawed glass, floated above him like balloons. The *chee-wee* cry receded a little. The tingling in his mind slacked off.

Rob tried to remember where he was. He couldn't.

He fought to remember. Bizarre colors chased through his head. Part of the name of the place surfaced in his mind. Star—

Star what?

Star*deep.*

But was he here?

Something in the past. Some reason he should know—

Try as he would, he couldn't remember.

Words, concepts, memories slipped away just as it seemed he was about to grasp them. He lay panting for breath in the center of the mall, while his brain buzzed and the balloon-faces drifted overhead. He grew panicky, thrashed his arms. He tried to recall where he had come from. He couldn't. His mind operated in slow motion, fogged, full of odd colors and sounds. He grew genuinely frightened.

He tried to raise himself to a sitting position. A tremendous wave of exhaustion swept over him, carrying him down toward billowy darkness.

The last image he held in his mind was that of the bearded man's face. It was a face oddly youthful despite the weather-beaten skin and hirsute covering.

Hateful, the blue chips of eyes burned, blazed, accused him of—what? He didn't know.

Then even that image faded. He stopped struggling and let the billowy dark cover him over.

# Nine

## MR. LUMMUS INSISTS

Toward the end of that same afternoon Rob awakened in a pale, aseptic room in what turned out to be the dispensary of the Conpat dome.

He discovered that he had nothing on except a pair of coarse hospital boxer shorts. He was lying in the scented slow-moving water of a hydrobed. On the wall opposite, the electronic letters of a diagnostic plaque spelled out:

*Edison, R. Inpatient (temp.) Condition: recup/normal.*
*Release: immed.*

From one side of the hemispherical bath-bed, Simon Ling and his daughter watched as Rob came back to full consciousness.

He thrashed the water as he sat up. "What happened?"

"Nothing too serious," Simon answered. "You just had your first experience with an Empt."

Rob flexed his arms, bent his knee in the tepid liquid. "I feel all right. My head aches a little, that's all."

"The diagnosis machines probed you for over half an hour," Lyndsey informed him. "Then they shot you full of a relaxant that made you sleep for two more."

The Commander indicated the lighted plaque. "You're free to go whenever you want. Your clothes are over there behind that floating screen."

Gently Rob eased himself out of the hemisphere. Trailing scented water from his heels, he moved behind the screen. He threw his soggy shorts into a chute and dressed. Once again his clothes were warm from a sonic cleaning. At this rate he was going to be the most germproof visitor on Stardeep.

As he tugged on his shirt, Rob remembered the wild montage of images that had flashed through his mind as he writhed on the turf of the mall.

"I got a strong dose of Empt mental energy, is that it?" he called.

"Correct," Simon replied from the other side of the screen. "You Empted."

"I could remember who I was, and where I was. But it was a struggle. I couldn't remember why I'd come to Stardeep, though."

"Everything unpleasant in your past was masked out of your mind," said Simon. "Now you understand why the Empts are so valuable in treating people who are mentally ill."

Rob shivered. His father, *Majestica*, the reason for his journey here—for that short time it had all been wiped away by the curious tingling emanations from the small squealing ball of life.

"I'll say."

Another memory slipped into place—the angry bluechip eyes of the bearded man.

"Who was that guy chasing the Empt, Commander? His owner?"

Rob thought his ears had tricked him when Lyndsey replied, "Footloose."

"What did you say?"

"The owner of the Empt is called Footloose," the Commander explained. "No one knows his right name. He's a Terran and very likely a lunatic. He's been living out on the reservation for years. You probably didn't notice, but the close association with the Empts has scrambled his speech. Since well before I got here, the Conpats have tolerated him, because he does no great harm. Once we tried to get him to come into this dispensary for treatment. He got so violent we decided it would be better to leave him alone."

Rob moved out from behind the screen, which promptly collapsed and folded itself into a slot in the wall. "And the Empt I caught is his pet?"

"One of the few pets we allow," Simon nodded.

"What was this Footloose character doing in town?"

Lyndsey provided the answer. "He comes to Churchill for supplies every month or so."

Simon grinned at Rob. "Your motives were noble, anyway."

Rob responded with a smile of his own. "Talk about a psychedelic experience!"

In his imagination he saw again the leathery, young-old face of the man called Footloose. He remembered particularly the malevolent glare of those blue-chip eyes. He mentioned this to the others.

Simon Ling pulled out his musicpipe and tobacco ball, which he inserted in the bowl. Pungent smoke and antique Brahms filled the sterile room as he replied, "Footloose showed up here too. He was still raging. By then we had rounded up his Empt for him. Two of my men got knocked out just the way you did while they caught the beastie. There's just no other way to capture an Empt. Drugsprays won't work. That's the reason Conpats have to be tough. It takes something out of a man to go through the Empting experience five or six times a day whenever we thin the reservation. Anyway, Footloose came storming in here. He seemed to think you were responsible for his Empt escaping. It was quite a scene. But I told you what kind of person he was—"

With a shake of his head, Simon used his pipestem to describe the age-old corkscrew sign of lunacy.

"Can I check out now?" Rob said.

"Anytime," Simon replied.

They left the room, headed down a corridor that led eventually to the Commander's office. Simon halted at the entrance.

Lyndsey said, "Dad tried to tell Footloose that you were helping to catch the Empt, and not the other way around. Dad explained who you were, a visitor to Stardeep, unfamiliar with the creatures—"

"Funny thing about that," Simon remarked from behind a soaring string passage and a cloud of smoke. "When I mentioned who you were—Rob Edison, a visitor from Dellkart IV—it seemed to work the poor coot up even more. He turned positively white, and that's not easy for a man who lives outdoors all year. Well, I suppose it was all due to his fear that we'd hurt his Empt or wouldn't let him have it again. We've already mended the chain. Man and Empt are on their way back to the reservation. We have to carry him over the barrier in a special short-hop flyer whenever he shows up. Nuisance."

"You need to be kind to someone like that, Dad," Lyndsey said. "I feel sorry for him. He really doesn't seem like a very old man."

"He isn't. Except inside his mind. Well, Rob—" A thick-fingered hand fell on Rob's shoulder in comradely fashion. "If you're feeling fit enough to navigate on your own"—Rob told them he was—"Lyndsey and I will say good-by for the day. We have some errands before mealtime. Your flyer is on schedule. It'll be waiting for you at the yard tomorrow morning at 0930. You won't find it hard to interrogate the Phylex Station. Complete instructions are spelled out on the station's programmer. Drop in when you get back in the afternoon. I'll be anxious to know the results of the trip."

"Thank you, Commander," Rob said with gratitude. "For everything." He started away.

"Rob?"

He turned back. Lyndsey's smile made him feel wanted. She said, "Good fortune across Stardeep."

Simon noticed his daughter's rapt expression, chuckled. "A localism meaning good luck, Rob." He waved and disappeared into his office.

Rob hurried down the antique fixed-position stairs. He recalled the look in Lyndsey's eyes long after he had gone out into the late-slanting sunlight on Avenue Ursus. The more he thought about her, the better he felt.

He headed for the central caf and a quick meal. His encounter with the Empt had left him tired. He wanted to turn in at the hostel and have a long, sound sleep before traveling out to the Phylex Station tomorrow. Excitement was building inside of him.

That excitement was marred by a sudden feeling that he was being watched.

He turned carefully. He scanned the bustling early evening crowds. He saw no one he recognized.

With a shrug he walked on until he came to the caf, and went inside.

He emerged twenty minutes later. All the way back to his hostel, the feeling that he was being observed persisted. He spent a tenth of a minicredit at a papertape kiosk, even though he wasn't really interested in scanning the day's news on the reader back in his room. He wanted a chance to survey the streets again.

Again he saw no one he could regard as suspicious. He continued on to the hostel.

On the eve of his trip to the Phylex Station, he hoped for a sound, dreamless slumber. It wasn't to be. Squealing Empts chased through his dreams, pursued by bearded young-old men in filthy clothes. They cursed Rob's name and glared at him with blue-chip eyes brimming with inexplicable hate.

As Rob stepped from the hostel next morning at 0845, a voice hailed him.

"Over here, young master!"

With a start he recognized Lummus. The man was waving to him from an adjoining walkway.

Instantly Rob was wary. He shook his head to indicate haste. He turned, started in the opposite direction. Lummus came after him, catching up with a wheeze and a puff.

Rob spun aroun ` as Lummus crowded him into the dim arcade entrance of a cosmetics shop not yet opened for the day.

"Get out of my way," Rob growled. "I'm in a hurry."

"But I insist that we have a chat, young master. I do insist." Lummus' lenslike brown eyes were unfriendly. The twist of his mouth could just barely be termed a smile. "If you are thinking of calling for a civil officer, don't. Not if you value the personal safety of the charming young lady with whom you traveled around town yesterday."

The nape of Rob's neck crawled.

The travel agent's fat fingers played a silent tattoo on his heaving paunch. In the cool shadows of the arcade a female voice whispered an advertisement for the shop's cosmetics. The head of Barton Lummus seemed to float like a bearded melon in the gloom, repulsive, diabolical.

"Are you making threats about the Commander's daughter?" Rob blazed.

Again that greasy smile spread across the drooping lips. "Not idle ones, I assure you. Come, come, young master! Let's discuss this like men of experience. It has come to my attention that you have applied for a pass that will permit you to enter the Empt reservation."

"But no one knows that except the Commander!" Rob was completely mystified.

Lummus wagged a yellow-stained finger. "Tut-tut. No one knows except those who were in the Commander's office when application was made, plus those who were outside, armed with a bit of electronic eavesdropping equipment."

"You listened—"

"Quite right. I am interested in gaining entry to the reservation. What more natural than to set up my listening post near Headquarters? Frankly, I had expected to wait days. Weeks! What a stroke of luck, eh, young master? A person with whom I am already acquainted turns up promptly and obtains permission!" Lummus' remarkably strong hand shot out to grip Rob's wrist. "You do have the flyer control card, do you not?"

Now Rob recalled something else. He shot back, "You mean the card you tried to pick out of my pocket?"

"I almost got it, too."

"You left a fingerprint."

Lummus let go of Rob's hand with a wounded sneer.

"What's this all have to do with Lyndsey Ling?" Rob demanded.

"She is merely my little device to ensure your cooperation. This morning, after her father left their domidome, my android Blecho and I slipped inside and—ah—requested her presence. At this moment my green-skinned companion is waiting with the girl at the park near the flyer compound. No one will question us if you have the pass card, you see. Thus we shall all be going out into the waste. Myself, that merciless rascal Blecho, Miss Ling, and you and your card."

"You kidnapped Lyndsey?" Rob was almost sputtering.

"Harsh words. But accurate."

"You're not a travel agent, are you? You're nothing but a cheap—"

Lummus struck Rob's cheek viciously hard. *"Be silent!"*

For an instant the fat man's face showed naked rage. Then he brought his emotions under control. He resumed that insufferable smirking and clamped his hand on Rob's shoulder again.

"Please be clear about it, young master. Unless you do as I say, the girl will be hurt." Barton Lummus sucked in a long, rattling breath. "Shall we go?"

# Ten

## DANGER FLIGHT

The walkways carried them toward the edge of town. Rob had the feeling that what was happening wasn't real.

Lummus chattered, commenting on the breezy morning weather, the architecture of Churchill which he held in contempt, the provincial mores and attitudes of the residents of Stardeep, and other miscellaneous topics.

Several times Rob asked pointed questions in a voice that betrayed his anxiety. What was Lummus' motive for this scheme? Where did he come from? What would happen when they took the flyer into the waste?

Lummus' response was invariably the same. He would jog his melon head to indicate people riding the other way.

"Privacy, young master! Ask your questions when we have privacy."

A few of the workers on their way into town gave Rob and his companion sharp stares. With his untidy clothing and jiggling chin beard, Lummus was a rather unusual sight. Each time he was noticed, Lummus fixed a smile on his face and nodded fatuously at the curious person on the other belt.

"Must maintain the front, mustn't we?" he said from a corner of his mouth. "Dear old uncle and nephew out for a morning excursion, what?"

Rob felt like snapping back with a sarcastic remark that Lummus wouldn't be mistaken for anybody's dear old uncle. But he didn't. Under the fat man's posturings, Rob sensed a core of ruthlessness.

The walkway carried them past a series of materials-handling domes. Ahead, lemon sunlight glared from the sides of pink-veined rocks.

On the other side of the park Rob glimpsed a flyer standing in the center of the compound. In vain he searched the area for a Conpat to whom he could turn for help. The servodome dock was empty.

The walkway bore them relentlessly on toward the platform alongside the park. Rob couldn't see Lyndsey or the android anywhere in the jumble of rocks.

All at once, as they were about to step off the way, Rob had an idea. He hung back, let Lummus precede him onto the platform. For an instant the obese man's back was turned. Rob stabbed his right hand inside his jacket. He seized the gray embossed card, yanked it out, started to drop it into the crack between the undulating belt and the platform.

Lummus whirled around. He shot out a porcine hand, dug his fingers deep into Rob's wrist. The gray card dropped from Rob's fingers. Lummus' other hand was already beneath it.

He caught the card. Then he pulled Rob hard, so that he nearly tumbled onto the platform on his face.

When Rob got his balance, Lummus thrust the card at him and glared.

"You dropped this, I believe? If you drop it again, young master, the young lady will be in for an extended stay in the dispensary. Or worse."

The point wasn't lost on Rob. Miserably, he shoved the gray card back into his jacket. He followed Lummus down the ramp to the park.

Still no one stirring at the flyer compound. His mind churned. Somehow he had to break out of this trap! But he didn't know how to do it.

He grew even less inclined to try something rash when he caught sight of Lyndsey Ling and the android. They appeared from behind one of the huge pink-veined rocks and came down a winding path. Lummus waved cheerily. Rob's stomach flipflopped. Lyndsey's cheeks were pale, her eyes wide and frightened. She stumbled when she recognized him.

Walking right behind her, the emerald android extended one hand from beneath a neutral cape that covered him from neck to knee, caught Lyndsey's elbow, and kept her upright with a rude jerk. Lyndsey's anger was apparent, but it melted under the frightening, almost inhuman stare of the android's blank eyes.

Lummus lumbered up to them. "Ah, good morning again, young mistress. How goes it, Blecho?"

"She wants to fight," remarked Blecho in a tinny voice.

"But not too vigorously, what?" To Rob, Lummus said, "I had Blecho put on that cloak for a special reason. Notice that my android has but one hand showing? His other, concealed, is clasped around an antique but nevertheless operative laser beam. In the event that it becomes necessary to combat violence with violence, he is a tip-top marksman."

"At close range," Blecho commented, "it is virtually impossible to miss."

"Quite so. Well, I believe your flyer is waiting, young master. Come along!"

Blecho led the way. Lyndsey fell in step alongside Rob. She whispered almost hysterically, "Do you know what's going on?"

"I wish I did. They want to go into the desert and my flyer card is their ticket." He noticed a bruise on her arm, just below the short sleeve of her pale-gold outfit. "Did they hurt you?"

"They frightened me half to death with that laser beam when they showed up at the dome after Dad left. Otherwise I'm all ri—"

"I find your whispers annoying," interrupted Lummus. "Desist, if you don't mind."

Lyndsey brushed back a lock of her straw-colored hair. She looked flushed now, and more than a little fearful. Rob admired the way she kept that fear under control.

They left the park and crossed the narrow strip of turf that was the boundary of the flyer compound. Blecho marched straight toward the teardrop flyer. Its hatch was open, its boarding ladder down. Suddenly a mech with a checkboard poked his head around the corner of the servodome dock.

"Morning," the mech called to Rob. "You Mr. Edison?"

"Yes." Desperately he tried to think of a way to call attention to their predicament.

The mech noticed Lyndsey. "Miss Ling! You going along too?"

"That's right, Tom," the girl returned with only a slight hesitation.

Lummus continued to smile blandly, as though his presence were perfectly normal. The mech consulted his checkboard, frowned. "The Commander didn't note down anything about other people in your party, Mr. Edison."

A lump clogged Rob's throat. Here was his chance. He was about to speak, when he noticed the emerald android leaning against the side of the flyer.

The craft was between the android and the servodome. The mech could not see Blecho move the hand slit of his cloak aside and thrust out a needle muzzle with a silver ball at its tip.

Blecho's blank gray eyes were turned to Rob, inhumanly sentient. The silver ball moved to point at Lyndsey.

"These are all friends of mine," Rob said. "The Commander knew we were going out together. Maybe—he just forgot about it."

The mech nodded. "Doesn't matter as long as you have the pass card."

"I do." Rob took it from his pocket, held it up.

The mech seemed satisfied. "Just put it in the marked slot. The flyer will do the rest. Good fortune across Stardeep!"

The mech waved his checkboard and vanished back inside the servodome.

"All aboard!" exclaimed Lummus with disheartening joviality.

The forecabin of the flyer was a dim oval. Padded benches curved around the outer sides. Lummus and the android sat on the benches to starboard. The fat man indicated that Lyndsey and Rob should sit facing them on the port side.

In spite of the complexity of dials and gauges spread on the control panel beneath the front viewplates, Rob had no difficulty spotting the place where the card was to be inserted. A red metal housing occupied a central position on the dash. Large enameled arrows above and below pointed to its horizontal slot. With a perspiring hand he slipped the gray card into the opening.

Immediately there was a clicking, a whining. The boarding ladder began to fold up. Rob took his seat beside Lyndsey.

The hatch whooshed shut and sealed its gasket. Thrusters sputtered. Air made a thin screaming sound as it filled the landing skids and burst out through the tiny openings on the undersides, raising the flyer off the ground. The thrusters cut in at full power. The flyer rose up from the yard in a smooth curve.

The craft banked out across the floor of the waste toward the purple peaks. Rob had an oblique view of the electronic barrier shimmering below them. It was quickly gone. The flyer leveled, turning away from the sun. The forecabin smelled of dust and oil.

Barton Lummus searched in his blouse for a sheaf of papers. He unfolded them, fixed his brown eyes on what appeared to be some sort of squiggly blue diagram.

Blecho looked totally uninterested. The tip of the laser beam had disappeared again beneath his cloak. Because his eyes lacked pupils, it was impossible to tell whether he was staring directly at the two prisoners. But Rob had the feeling that he was.

"Rob?"

He turned, startled anew by the raw fear in Lyndsey's eyes.

"Do you know who these men are?"

"Mr. Lummus came to Stardeep on the same ship I did," Rob told her. "He said he was a travel agent. I should have trusted my first reaction—all bad."

"It's a splendid cover, though," remarked Lummus affably. "The bureaucratic clods staffing the law enforcement agencies of the various worlds to which my affairs take me never question it."

"Don't you think it's time you told us what this is all about?" Rob asked.

Lummus shrugged. "I see no reason why not. The answer is Empts."

Lyndsey blinked. "Did I hear you correctly? You said—"

"Empts." Lummus grew sarcastic. "You are familiar are you not, with those little beggars your father and his officious assistants guard so assiduously? People want Empts desperately. Especially neurotic persons who don't wish to bare their intermost problems to a psychomed. With their remarkable facility for obliterating all past traumas, Empts are in constant demand on the various planetary gray markets with which I have—ah—connections. I have come to Stardeep with a group of assistants to help myself to several dozen Empts and thereby increase the size of my computerized financial holdings."

"A poacher!" Lyndsey breathed.

"A good one," observed the expressionless android. "Best that ever hired me."

"Faithful beggar," Lummus said, patting the android's shoulder. "Blecho has a passion for immersing himself in low-viscosity industrial lubricants. It's akin to the human sport of swimming in natural water. Also, Blecho's manufacturer scrambled his enzyme balance. As a result, he has absolutely no scruples about murdering anyone who obstructs—"

"Can we skip that kind of talk?" Rob cut in.

"Oh, I am sorry, young master."

But he wasn't in the least. His thrust had been well calculated to terrify Lyndsey Ling even more. Her expression showed that it had succeeded.

Lummus rattled the sheaf of papers. "These, plus my ability to penetrate the Empt reservation, will be the secrets of my success on this little venture. The electronic barriers around the reservation are plaguing problems, I don't mind telling you. Especially the sky barrier ten miles up. That barrier prevents any ship from coming straight down onto the reservation. It is controlled, however, by ground-based circuitry. These"—again the sheaf rattled—"were obtained at great expense from the gray market on Ketchum's Cloudplanet. Schematics of the circuitry of a three-square-mile area of the barrier in the sky. The power station controlling this part of the barrier is located approximately eight miles overland from the Phylex Monitor installation at which we'll land. Thus I needed to get inside the barrier without detection—"

"So you could reach the power station," Rob concluded.

"How perspicacious you are," Lummus replied with a faint sneer. "As soon as we are down, faithful Blecho and I shall travel to the power station, disrupt the circuits, and thus eliminate the aforementioned portion of the barrier. I have a ship out in orbit at this very moment, manned by an excellent crew of poachers. The ship will come down through the opening in the barrier. We shall round up several dozen Empts and be away no later than nightfall—undetected!"

Beaming with self-congratulation, Lummus sat back and began to dust food specks from his trousers.

Lyndsey shuddered. "I think it's disgusting."

"Disgusting to turn a profit? What a quaint concept."

"Disgusting you'd steal Empts that could help really sick people."

Lummus raised a porky hand. "Spare me the pious Conpat propaganda, if you please."

All through the conversation, Rob had been thinking about possible courses of action. He saw that they were approaching the purple mountains, a saw-toothed, deep-colored rampart. They had been flying not much more than ten minutes, but already the thrusters were changing pitch. A sudden hissing indicated that the landing skid aircushions were going into action.

The flyer lost altitude. The downtilt of the teardrop bow told him they would be landing shortly.

Blecho pointed at the port. "Phylex Station."

Rob saw it coming up among the rocky foothills in a rush: a three-story column of chrome alloy rising from a stressed concrete base. A circular liftstair wound round and round the outside of the column. It led the eye upward to the station itself, a transparent bubble at the column's top. Inside the bubble Rob glimpsed machinery.

Lummus put away his diagrams. "A most pleasant trip, wouldn't you say? You will accompany us to the power station, young master. As soon as my ship lands and we round up a sufficient number of Empts, you will be on your own. We shall leave you in the waste to be rescued by the Conpats at some later time. You won't starve. At least I don't believe you will," the fat man concluded.

"Tonight Dad will discover we're gone—" Lyndsey began hopefully.

"And I shall be gone also," Lummus said. "Happy thought, what?"

"Be very rich," Blecho remarked to no one in particular. "Go to another planet. Bathe in oil for a week."

The flyer was settling in an open area surrounded by large purple boulders. The base of the nearby Phylex tower was hidden by the rocks. Behind the column-and-bubble, the rock-strewn land sloped upward to the sharp angle where sheer purple cliffs began.

There was a tilt, a crunch, as the flyer landed on rocky ground. The thrusters cut out. The hatch unsealed with a whisper. Clanging, the hatch flew back. Lemon sunlight and a warm, dusty-smelling wind flooded in.

The boarding stair unfolded. Carefully Rob stood up. He took Lyndsey's hand, pulled her after him. She forced a smile. But her bright-blue eyes were getting a glazed look. No wonder, with Blecho's laser beam an obvious lump beneath his cloak.

Rob felt hot as he edged toward the hatch. He studied the ground outside. It was covered with a heavy pumice. Here and there lay egg-sized or larger stones, all various shades of purple. He spotted one near the embedded lower prongs of the ladder. A tic began to beat in his cheek. He averted his head as Lummus clumped past.

The fat man was intent on the landscape outside. He surveyed it with a gross, lip-smacking satisfaction. His straggly chin beard blew back and forth in the breeze as he stepped to one side at the hatch.

"You first, Blecho."

The android plodded outside, started down the stairs. Lummus signed for Rob and Lyndsey to follow. Blecho was four steps from the bottom as Rob ducked through and dug his heels into the top step. The lemon sun beat into his eyes. He swallowed hard and jumped.

*"Blecho!"* Lummus howled as Rob sailed down on top of the android and bashed his fist on top of the hairless emerald head.

Blecho uttered a cry in some alien dialect, collapsing under Rob's weight. Rob rolled off to one side. The android floundered. Things happened with confusing swiftness.

"The beam, the beam, you stupid construct!" Lummus shouted. Rob saw a flash of silver in the sun. Blecho had lost his grip on the laser beam. It was on the ground lying in the open.

Barton Lummus bounded down the boarding stairs, knocking Lyndsey aside. The android seemed confused, as though Rob's blow had impaired its thinking. It rubbed an emerald hand back and forth over its brow. All pretense of gentility gone, Lummus booted Blecho out of the way and dove for the laser beam.

Simultaneously, Rob closed his hand around the purple stone he had noticed before. A stone against an old-fashioned but deadly lightweapon was, he realized, not very much of a contest.

# Eleven

## "A TOUCH OF THE LASER"

Barton Lummus swung the ball-tipped muzzle of the laser beam on a direct line with Rob's stomach. Rob had never been so frightened in his life.

He didn't stop to think. Faster than he could have imagined, he flung the stone.

It struck Lummus in the forehead. The fat man howled. A gash opened in his forehead, leaking blood. Lummus swore and hopped from foot to foot.

Shoulder tucked low, Rob charged.

He dodged in past the weapon and hit Lummus' stomach. The fat man toppled backward, wigwagging his arms. His gasp sounded like a balloon deflating. By that time Rob was racing past the android.

Blecho made an abortive lunge, but Rob's footwork, fast as a gravball court maneuver, helped him slip neatly around behind the green creature.

Lyndsey gaped at him from the boarding stair. Rob reached up, caught her hand, pulled her down toward him.

He braced himself as she tumbled against him. He kept her from falling, wound his fingers tightly around hers, and started to run.

The glazed look disappeared from Lyndsey's eyes. Her straw-colored hair streamed as she struggled to match Rob's pace. Behind, Rob heard Barton Lummus venting his anger with all sorts of swearwords. The fat man interrupted the profanity to screech at Blecho to get moving.

The pumice chopped hard against the soles of Rob's sandals. Lyndsey's breathing was loud in his ear. They reached the large purple boulders behind which Rob meant to take cover.

Rob banged into the first boulder, scraping his shoulder. He started around behind the rock, still dragging Lyndsey by the hand. She cried out. The pressure of her fingers vanished.

Rob spun around. Lyndsey was being dragged backward by the android.

Blecho had his hands locked around the girl's waist from behind. When she started to kick, the android lifted her off the ground.

Panicked, Rob headed back around the rock toward Lyndsey and her captor. He was just passing the boulder when a thin beam of ruby light sliced past his ear and silently disintegrated a section of the big rock.

The circular depression smoked and stank of ozone. There was a brief aftercrackle of sound. Instinctively Rob ducked his head, jumped backward so that the boulder hid him.

Heart beating furiously, he lay with one cheek against the rough, cool stone.

That laser beam could have killed him!

After a moment he managed to calm down. He heard the sounds of a struggle from the other side of the rock, grew furious with himself for reacting without thinking. He should have charged straight ahead, not backward into cover. Now he was separated from Lyndsey, Blecho, and Lummus by the massive rock.

"Young master?" Lummus' pebbly voice was fragmented by the breeze. "Can you hear me?"

"I hear you," Rob called.

"I meant that as a warning. Poaching is one matter, homicide another entirely. I do not wish to have one or more deaths on my record. However"—Lummus panted between words—"you force me to extreme measures. Blecho has the girl in his grasp again. If you persist in balking me—"

Angry, Rob flung a stone over the top of the boulder.

From the other side Blecho croaked in alarm. The stone struck and rattled. Rob shook his head, a savage motion.

This was getting him absolutely nowhere. Lyndsey was a prisoner, and it was up to him to keep a cool head. Losing his temper because he had reacted normally and gone for cover wouldn't help the situation. He forced himself to crouch down behind the rock and await developments.

Almost at once, Lummus bawled, "One more trick like that, and I'll give the young lady a touch of the laser."

A pause. The wind blew in gusts, whining around the boulders.

"Do you realize that I'm perfectly serious, young master? Too much is at stake—"

"All right!" was Rob's reply. "Just don't hurt her."

"What happens to her depends entirely on you."

"What do you mean?"

"You force a change in my plans. I cannot afford to be on guard against your tactics every inch of the way from here to the power station. Therefore, since it seems that I have you temporarily bottled up"—a chuckle—"I believe I will simply leave you where you are."

Another flurry of sound. Rob recognized Lyndsey's voice. Blecho complained, "This girl is kicking me."

"Kick her back, you simpleton," Lummus snarled. Lyndsey's cries subsided.

"Pay attention, you young whelp," Lummus called after a moment. "My companion and I will proceed overland to the power station. We will take the girl with us. Now I warn you, don't come after us. If I so much as see your ear sticking out from behind a rock, I will take steps. Yes."

Lummus' voice lowered. Rob didn't miss the new, more sinister timbre. The fat man was reacting to the frustration of his plan, and reacting in an ugly way.

"If you pursue us, this little lady will get that touch of the laser I mentioned. Nothing fatal. Just enough to cripple her. A foot, a hand—a touch will do it nicely."

Rob's flesh crawled. He swallowed hard, kept silent.

"Did you hear what I said, young master?"

All Rob could answer was, "Yes. Lummus—don't hurt her." *A touch of the laser.* The words made Rob's stomach hurt. He called out, "Lyndsey?"

Her voice was faint. "W—what?"

"I'll do what he says. Don't fight and they won't hurt you."

"We can't let him steal a fortune in Empts—"

"It doesn't matter!" Rob cried vehemently. "You're more important than—"

"Not to me she isn't," Lummus interrupted. "And don't you forget it."

Another pause. The wind blew eerily around the boulders. Rob felt hopelessly trapped.

"We're going now," Lummus informed him, above the moan of the wind.

All at once Rob knew that he couldn't allow Barton Lummus to carry Lyndsey off to the power station without making an effort to rescue her. He would give them a good head start. Then, as carefully as possible, he would follow.

He had to do it! Lummus, in his excited state and with a huge potential profit at stake, might dispose of the girl, anyway, if she proved an encumbrance. And Rob knew he would go crazy if he simply sat for hours without doing anything.

Let Lummus think he had won the point. That might throw him off guard. Then—what?

Well, he'd figure something. He had to.

Breathing a little more steadily, Rob settled down to wait.

From the opposite side of the boulder drifted the faint sound of the party setting out. Lummus gave orders to Blecho. The android responded with another complaint. Lummus raised his voice. The android didn't reply.

Rob heard Lyndsey ask the android not to hold her arm so tightly. Lummus grudgingly ordered his companion to treat her a little less roughly. Feet rattled in the pumice—Lummus' heavy, dragging step, the lighter scrape of Lyndsey's sport shoes, the stolid, rhythmic clump-clomp of the android. Soon the keen of the wind obliterated the sounds altogether.

Cautiously Rob crawled out from behind the boulder. He found a rock he could scale, clambered to the top, searched the foothills.

The sun was moving up toward zenith, shedding bright light on the faces of the purple mountains. The bubble at the top of the Phylex column glittered like a jewel. Rob turned his gaze outward—southward, he calculated it would be—from the mountains.

Off to the southwest, an uninterrupted vista of boulder-strewn foothills, a puff of dust rose. Lummus and the others were moving roughly parallel to the base of the mountain chain. At least now he knew the right direction.

He watched for several moments longer, making sure from repeated drifts of the dust that he was right. He was. There was no other sign of life anywhere.

Directly south, the waste leveled off, dun-colored, un-friendly. One hundred and ten miles back there lay help. If only he could contact—

But he could.

Irritated by his slow thinking, Rob scrambled down from the boulder and raced to the teardrop flyer.

The forecabin was cool after the heat of the wind. He started with the ceiling monitors and controls. He read the nameplate of each. Nothing of significance.

He moved to the starboard side of the complex dash panel. Again he scanned the nameplates one by one. SKID P.S.I. FUEL MIX. RIGHT GUIDE VANES. LEFT GUIDE VANES. He growled in frustration, kept reading.

Suddenly he spotted a green servoswitch over toward the port side of the panel. The nameplate read DISTRESS BEACON.

Rob threw the switch to the ON position.

He thought he detected a faint vibration in the hull and floorplates. He wondered about the nature of the beacon. An ultrasonic, maybe? No way of telling. But he hoped that whatever the signal the teardrop craft emitted, it would be picked up back in Churchill.

As he left the cabin, a sudden flare of light up to his left caught his eye.

From the top of the Phylex Monitor bubble, a spidery antenna had extended. Its basketwork dish made one revolution every few seconds. Rob managed a grin. Perhaps the rescue craft from Churchill would home in on that.

Outside the flyer, Rob checked the ground. He discovered that by leaning his weight into every step, he could leave definite impressions in the pumice. Therefore he could afford to wait a few more minutes before starting after Lummus and the others. By taking care to leave tracks, he would give the Conpats a trail to follow.

He felt a little better. Now he was getting some results.

He sat down in the shade of a large rock to wait five minutes. He timed the interval by observing the rotation of the antenna high up on the bubble. Four minutes passed. He heard a sudden scurrying noise in the rocks.

The palms of his hands turned cold. Could it be an Empt? He listened harder.

Footsteps. Heavy footsteps. Slipping and scrunching through the pumice.

Lummus didn't trust him! He had sent Blecho back to spy, or had come himself.

Sweat broke out on Rob's face and arms. He eased himself to his feet, began to creep around the boulder in the direction of the intruder.

All at once he doubted that it was Lummus or his android henchman. Neither one would make so much noise.

He frowned, backed against the rock. In another second, whoever it was would come through the narrow opening between this boulder and the next. Fingers dug tight into his palms, Rob waited.

*Scrunch-scrape. Slide-crunch.* Someone was humming, off key.

A spindly human shadow spilled across the pumice near Rob's feet. He heard a soft clinking. A smaller, spherical shadow split off from the larger one. Rob held his breath.

Out from between the boulders shot three translucent pseudopods. A second later, the rest of the Empt followed. There was a staple in its back. A light alloy chain clinked against its plating. *Chee-wee! Chee-wee!*

And then Rob was staring into the wild and astonished blue eyes of the man called Footloose.

# Twelve

## RESCUE PLAN

Footloose reacted instantly. He shuffled backward two steps, fisted his free hand, and raised it over his head to threaten Rob, his face contorted, hostile.

The Empt rushed to its master, cowered against the man's bare, callused foot. *Chee-wee,* the creature cried. Its faceted eyes glowed gold.

For one tense moment the scene held: Rob standing startled while Footloose waved his fist to and from above his head. Beneath the floppy brim of the bearded man's hat, the blue-chip eyes shone angrily.

"I won't hurt you," Rob said. "Don't you recognize me—?"

His words became a mumble. Footloose's face seemed to dissolve like gelatin. The outlines of the boulders, the purple peaks smeared.

Rob staggered back a step. The surroundings distorted even more.

The Empt continued its yelping cry. Rob's head tingled. The tingling spread to his jawbone. All at once he understood. He was in the Empt's zone of radiation.

Things grew more and more blurred. The ground tilted one way, then the other. Rob blinked hard. That didn't help.

Footloose took a step forward. His mouth cracked into a sly smile. He had Rob on the run.

The boy turned. He used all his energy to take a staggering step, then another. Footloose cackled. "Scared, you. I scared you good, didn't I, person?"

The half-maniacal voice dinned in Rob's ears. He

seemed to be sluicing through hip-deep liquid. The air itself showed weird ripples and bends.

Rob plowed ahead. The tingling in his skull diminished. He kept going until he was a good twenty feet from the bearded man, who had stopped in the shade of a boulder and lowered his fist.

Breath came heavy in Rob's lungs. He felt as if he were surfacing from a long underwater dive. Gradually the silhouettes of the peaks sharpened. The waviness vanished from the air. At last the tingling faded altogether.

Rob wiped an arm across his mouth. He tasted the saltiness of his own skin. Sucking deep gulps of air, he turned around.

*Chee-wee,* cried the Empt. It was still tucked against its master's anklebone. It resembled an armored ball now. No pseudopods were showing.

Footloose grinned even wider. He clinked the length of the light alloy chain rapidly in both hands.

"My critter won't hurt you, person. I will, though."

Rob shook his head, swallowed. He felt almost normal. But he wasn't certain about how to deal with the stranger.

Footloose had one foot planted out in front of him. The posture was almost defiant. He pushed back his cone-crowned hat. Tangled hair on his forehead spilled out. His teeth shone like bits of ivory. His blue-chip eyes crinkled at the corners, unnaturally lively.

Rob tried a simple gambit. "I'm your friend."

"No friends here." Footloose waved the chain at the mountains. "All alone."

"But I know your name."

That surprised the bearded man. "You do?"

"It's Footloose, right? You live out here all by yourself with your Empt."

The statement made the man wary again. "Who told you about me? About my critter?"

"I met you in Churchill."

The stranger considered this even more astonishing. "Where I go for victuals?"

"That's right. Last time you were there, your—critter—escaped."

Emphatically Footloose shook his head. "Never happened, person. I'd remember."

"You don't remember chasing your Empt down the mall? I caught it for you."

"Never happened," Footloose repeated. He took a few steps forward. Rob countered with an equal number of steps to the rear. Again Footloose reacted with that child-like expression of astonishment. "Why you stand away off there, person?"

"Because if I get too close to your Empt, I'll forget what happened just before you showed up." The way you obviously forgot your Empt running away in Churchill, Rob added to himself.

Rob studied Footloose more closely. It was impossible to tell his age. The man's skin, especially his forehead and the backs of his hands, were rough-textured from long exposure to the open air of Stardeep. In the right light, his deep suntan appeared to have an ebony sheen. All that suggested age. So did the gray streakings in his beard. And yet the blue-chip eyes were oddly youthful. Footloose might be anywhere from twenty-five to forty-five years old.

The stranger hooked his eyebrows together, trying to concentrate on what was clearly a serious matter. "Something bad has happened here, person?"

"My name is Edison, not person." Rob was annoyed at having to deal with the stranger's slow mental processes. He gestured to the scuffed pumice. "There was a fight. I came here with a girl whose father is Commander of the Conpats—"

"Conpats are good men," Footloose said with a genuine smile. "They let me live out here. They carry me over the shocking walls and back when I need victuals."

A plan suggested itself suddenly. "Then you should help me, Footloose," Rob said.

"Help you do what, Edison person?"

"Help me get the girl back from the men I was fighting. They're bad men." He stressed it with an exaggerated face. "Very, very bad." The effect drew a response. Footloose scowled. Rob went on: "One of the men has a laser beam. He may use it to hurt the Conpat Commander's daughter. The men are trying to steal Empts—"

Footloose bent swiftly to scoop up his pet. He cradled the armored creature in the crook of one elbow and patted its plates with his other hand.

"Take mine?" he asked, worried.

"They might. They'll take any they can get."

"Not allowed," Footloose growled. "My friends Conpats say no."

"But the Conpats aren't here, Footloose. We're the only ones who can stop the men. They took the girl to a power station over that way. Do you know where it is?"

"Know, Edison person," Footloose nodded.

"Then will you help me? I think you and your Empt and I could get the girl away."

Footloose gnawed his cracked lower lip. "Not sure you're a friend."

"I helped save your Empt in Churchill!"

The bearded man passed a hand in front of his eyes, a vague gesture. "Not sure."

"Because you've forgotten! The Empt erased—oh, never mind."

Rob was conscious of the changing angle of the lemon sun. Minutes were slipping by while he argued with this naïve hermit. He put as much pleading into his voice as he could muster.

"Believe me, Footloose, I wouldn't take your Empt. But those men I talked about would. If they get hold of your pet, you'll never see him—it—again."

Footloose sniffed, disdainful of Rob's ignorance. He stroked the creature's plates. It let out a faint *chee-wee*.

"It's a lady, don't you know?"

"I beg her pardon and yours. Will you help?"

After some deliberation, Footloose asked, "What must be done, Edison person?"

Quickly Rob explained what he had in mind. Footloose did not grasp all the details right away. Rob had to go over certain parts two and three times. When he finished, Footloose still gave no sign of being willing. His blue-chip eyes gleamed suspiciously from under the grimy brim of his hat.

"The Lummus person is the one with the hurting thing?" he asked.

"Yes, the laser beam."

"Will he hurt my critter with it?"

"Not if the plan works right."

"You swear Lummus person means to steal Empts?"

"Dozens of them," Rob avowed.

"You say you helped me in Churchill—" Footloose still looked a little dubious. Then, abruptly, the lines of his face smoothed out. He was less menacing. "I believe you, Edison person. And all the talk about Conpat daughter and stealing Empts too. I'll help."

Weary from the long exchange, Rob almost whooped.

Footloose lowered his Empt gently to the ground. Kneeling in front of the creature, he extended his right hand.

Fascinated, Rob watched a chink appear in the Empt's plates. One pseudopod extended, translucent and quivering. Footloose laid his palm on top of the pseudopod. His beard danced in the wind as he made a face. It was an exaggerated grin, almost as though he were a grandfather trying to charm an infant into smiling. From deep in his throat, he brought forth a sound that was a very close imitation of the *chee-wee* cry.

He repeated the sound in varying rhythms. All at once the Empt retracted its pseudopod and began to roll back and forth. Footloose clapped his hands. He stood up, continuing to make the *chee-wee* sound, which the Empt immediately duplicated.

Listening to the cacophony, Rob blinked. "Footloose, can you talk to that thing?"

The bearded man peered over the shoulder of his sunbleached blouse. "Isn't a thing. It's a critter. Critters have brains like we have brains!" Footloose exclaimed. Rob was impressed by his depth of feeling for the odd beasts.

"Critter brains are little, so the Conpat persons tell me," Footloose went on. He showed how little by measuring off the ball of his thumb with his index finger, then enlarging the volume threefold by pantomiming with both hands. "But critters think and talk, person. I know it. I have lived with them always." Again that vague, peculiar gesture, as though Footloose were trying to brush cobwebs from his eyes. "Or at least I think always. Maybe part of always. Half. Some." He shrugged. "Anyway, Edison person, they listen to me. Know what I say."

Even better! Rob thought. He moved forward a few steps, carried by his own enthusiasm, but he recoiled sharply when the tingling started in the frontal bones of his head.

Back in a safe position beyond the reach of the Empt's power, he said, "Listen carefully, will you please, Footloose? Remember the plan I told you about?"

Footloose pondered, finally nodded. Score one, Rob thought. At least he doesn't consider that unpleasant. Yet. He continued. "Remember how I said we'd use your Empt against the men who took the girl? Well, more than one Empt would make it a lot easier."

Rob paused to give Footloose time to think it over. The man followed the concept with some difficulty. Even when he nodded and murmured, "More Empts easier." Rob wasn't sure he understood. But he pressed on, anyway.

"Could you round up some more Empts right now?"

"How many, person?"

"About half a doz—this many." Rob held up all the fingers on one hand.

Footloose's lips moved in silence as he counted. "Think so. Take time, though."

"Very much?" Rob was worried about more delay.

Footloose struggled for a way to express the time idea. At last he held up his own hand with three fingers raised. He added his little finger just to be certain.

"This much all right, Edison person?"

"If it's no longer," Rob agreed. He hoped Footloose meant minutes rather than hours or days.

"Be back," Footloose chortled, giving a tug to his Empt's chain. Man and creature vanished among the rocks.

Rob let out a long sigh. He wandered over to a shady place and hunched down.

Already the boulders were throwing off longer shadows. Atop the Phylex Station the spidery antenna continued to turn in silence. For a moment Rob felt very discouraged.

The threat posed by Lummus was diverting him from the purpose of his trip into the waste. He looked enviously at the bubble of the Phylex Station. How soon would he get back to interrogate its banked tapes?

He had to help Lyndsey Ling. But he was already so embroiled in this trouble that his week and a half on Stardeep might run out before he even had a chance to start his search.

It had been an alarming day. And he wasn't so sure he'd done the right thing by inviting the assistance of an obvious lunatic who—

*Chee-wee! Chee-wee!*

The cry up in the rocks startled him. He realized that it came from a human throat.

The sound echoed strangely on the shifting wind. It was repeated at intervals during the next few minutes. Then there was an answering cry. Another. Before long the slopes above the clearing rang with the squeals.

Was Footloose summoning Empts from the caves that

Simon Ling said were woven all through the peaks and foothills? It must be so.

In another moment, the scarecrow figure appeared along a defile, waving his cone-crowned hat and uttering the strange cry full volume. Footloose grinned so wide that his mouth looked like a porcelain ornament. Behind him, racing along by extending groups of three pseudopods, came six more Empts, four larger and two smaller than the pet that Footloose still had with him on his chain.

"All here," Footloose shouted. "I can get more, Edison person—"

Rob shook his head, which was already tingling. He started walking so as to keep well ahead of the little Empt army. He motioned for Footloose to follow.

"We help the Conpat girl, yes?" Footloose chortled, dancing along behind Rob like a macabre pied piper. "I am only afraid for one thing, person. That the Lummus uses his bad hurting thing on my critters."

Or on us, thought Rob grimly as he led the way from a safe distance.

Soon he, Footloose, and the chirruping Empts were moving through the foothills on a line parallel to the mountains. Footloose was completely cheerful again. Apparently the presence of his little friends relieved him of all worry about the possible peril ahead. Empting certainly had its advantages, Rob thought.

# Thirteen

## FIGHT AT THE POWER STATION

The trail to the power station wasn't difficult to follow. Barton Lummus had taken no trouble to hide his tracks, preferring, Rob supposed, to move swiftly and accomplish his objective as soon as possible. But covering the eight miles proved harder than Rob expected.

It soon became evident that Lummus had only the roughest idea of the terrain through which he was so obviously hurrying. The trail he left wound back and forth through the foothills. Rob discovered this when Footloose called to him from behind. The bearded man indicated a narrow crevice between two boulders. Rob shook his head, pointed to the footprints ahead. He felt it was imperative to keep to the trail in case anything happened to Lyndsey along the way.

Footloose argued in his half-coherent manner that the crevice was a shortcut. But Rob stuck to his original idea. With a grumble, Footloose squeaked to his Empts, who had a tendency to wander off whenever he didn't keep at them with a *chee-wee* cry every few seconds.

The lemon sun of Stardeep was far down toward the horizon when Footloose again called Rob's name. He was making erratic gestures.

Rob wiped sweat from his eyes. He was worn out from pushing across the up-and-down terrain of the sloping approaches to the mountains. He estimated that they had been on the march some three to four hours, and his sandals had offered next to no protection. His feet bled from half a dozen ugly gashes. To top it off, he was growing a little light-headed from lack of food.

"Not far now, Edison person," Footloose informed him with a wave. "Other side, there."

Rob willed himself to alertness. He was aware of the risk of shouting at Footloose across the intervening distance, so he tried making the traditional finger-to-lips gesture for silence, coupling it with gestures toward the ridge. Footloose seemed to understand.

"We go up and hide in the rocks at the top there, we see them," he said.

"Let me go first. You wait here."

Footloose ticktocked his head in a nonchalant way. His largest Empt started to scuttle away downhill. Footloose let out the *chee-wee* cry. Rob clapped his hands.

The sound reverberated among the rocks, too loudly. But Footloose got the idea. He grinned in a vacant way, sheepishly mimed the finger-to-lips.

Rob tried to keep his patience, returned the smile. Footloose squatted on his heels. He uttered his cry to the Empts again, but this time much more softly. The round creatures, including the runaway, gathered around his feet. He stroked each in turn.

Rob slipped between boulders, crept to the ridge. Here the shadows had lengthened. The constant breeze was turning cool. He found a shallow gully that seemed to offer fairly good footing as it wound to the crest.

As he stepped into the gully, his left foot slid against the edge of a sharp stone. He stifled a cry. Another gash opened, bleeding. He kept his mind on Lyndsey Ling and forgot the pain.

Near the top he dropped down flat on his stomach. He crawled the rest of the way. Slowly he lifted his head.

At least something was going right!

There, in a cuplike depression surrounded on three sides by boulders, stood the power station. It was nothing more than a large weatherproof plasto egg, perhaps eight feet on its long axis. Inside, he could see color-coded circuitry panels arranged like vertical folders on a shelf. The egg was mounted on a preformed concrete pedestal. And there were Lummus, Blecho, and—thank heaven!—Lyndsey.

The girl was between the station and the ridge, sprawled out on the ground with her hair a tangle in her eyes. Her one-piece garment that had looked so crisp this morning was now stained and torn. Lyndsey was on her side, an awkward position. Something that resembled the belt of

Barton Lummus' trousers was lashed round and round her wrists and ankles, pulling them tight together.

Lyndsey paid no attention to her captors. She stared with fixed expression at the natural entrance to the little depression. There, no boulders obstructed the view of the waste that shimmered in the late sun. From the girl's melancholy stare, Rob guessed that she must be incredibly weary and frightened.

Blecho and the bogus travel agent were quite busy. Two of the service doors in the transparent egg had been broken open. Several circuitry panels had been pulled out on extendable roller tracks. One group of panels at the egg's far end had already been fused into a shapeless mass. Now, at the end of the egg nearest Rob's hiding place, Blecho reached inside and slid a second panel out alongside another.

Lummus rattled his diagrams. "Not that one, you chemical cretin! The green-keyed one."

"Looks green to me," Blecho said, rapping his emerald knuckles against the yellow board.

"Just like the color of your hide, what?"

When Blecho nodded, Lummus sneered and reached past the android's shoulder. The fat man shoved the yellow board back inside on its track, pulled out the correct one.

"Someone should have issued a warranty when you were manufactured in that Draconian lab," he grumbled. "The shoddy workmanship is appalling. You've been seeing the wrong colors ever since we got here. Stand aside and let me finish it!"

Lummus' irritation hardly fazed the android. Blecho stood with folded arms while the fat man huffed and snorted and dragged forth two more boards of differing colors. He glanced quickly at his diagrams. Lummus' face was white with an accumulation of dust mixed with sweat. He began to fold the diagrams.

"Where's the cave map I gave you? I'll hang on to all the valuables."

From under his cloak the android produced another folded sheet. This, together with the diagrams, disappeared in Lummus' waistband.

"You fuse them," he ordered, lurching over to a stone and sitting down with a gargantuan puff.

Blecho drew out the laser beam. He turned it on and directed the thin ruby light at the four boards hanging out-

side the egg. The surfaces of the boards began to glisten
and spark.

Lummus picked up a pebble, played with it. "I'd like to
get my hands on the formula for the alloy those panels are
made from. I'd use it to build a sweet little ship so tough
that all the law chasers in the galaxy couldn't burn its
hull." He glanced at the darkening sky. It was streaked in
the northeast by the first gleamings of moonrise. A green
radiance touched the sawtooth peaks.

"As soon as those blasted boards melt, Blecho, the sky
barrier will open. How infernally much longer is it going to
take you?"

The android continued burning the panels. "Five or ten,
now."

"If Captain Ridirigo doesn't put the ship on the ground
within fifteen minutes after we knock out the barrier, I'll
have his hide. We're already behind schedule."

Emphasizing the cause, Lummus lobbed another pebble
toward Lyndsey. The pebble hit her shoulder from behind,
startling her. She let out a low, dismayed cry.

Rob scowled, fought his anger. Twists of smoke rose
from the extended panels now. The air reeked of ozone.
The aftercrackle of the intense red beam was continuous.
He had no more time to waste.

Rob started crawling backward down the gully. His sandal struck some loose stones. The rattling was loud in the
stillness.

He clutched the gully wall, didn't move. On the other
side of the ridge, Barton Lummus took instant notice.

"Blecho! Did you hear that noise?"

Evidently the android replied that he didn't. Rob
couldn't catch the answer above the faint aftercrackle of
the laser beam. But he distinctly heard Lummus, who
sounded relieved.

"Just one of those little Empt beggars, I suppose. My
nerves are in a state. I'm a sensitive person, Blecho. Not
being human, you fail to understand the effect of any dis-
ruption of my well-ordered plans. I didn't anticipate having
to hold that ridiculous girl hostage. Nor did I count on that
young master showing any spirit whatsoever. The youth
these days—its the same on all the planets—"

The rest of the grumping monologue was lost as Rob
continued his scramble back to the base of the ridge.

Footloose saw him coming. He rose. Rob pantomimed

his instructions. The third time through, Footloose seemed to understand.

Hoping the bearded man really did have the idea, Rob turned and began to climb. Near the top he slid into a gully, twisted his head around to look back.

Down below, Footloose had gathered the Empts. He was talking to them. Fortunately he kept his voice down.

The largest Empt, the one that had shown a tendency to wander, began to quiver suddenly. It emitted a quick series of cries. *Chee-wee, chee-wee.*

Rob slid up the ridgeline, peered over.

Blecho had nearly reduced the circuit panels to melted ruin. Barton Lummus was walking up and down. He halted when he heard the cry of the Empt.

"There *is* one of the beggars around here! One more for the bag, what? I'll go see."

Lummus started for the slope. His path would bring him up to the place where Rob was hiding. Rob's palms were slippery again. His heart raced.

Fortunately Footloose had done his job.

To the left, where the ridge sloped to the plain, the half dozen Empts were traveling with amazing speed. The largest Empt reached the natural entrance to the depression and shot through. The others followed.

Lummus gaped. "A veritable flock of the beggars! Fancy that!"

One of the little Empts raced toward the fat man's feet. Lummus blinked. Another Empt joined the first while two more converged on Blecho. And the android's pupilless eyes studied them. Rob watched tensely for a sign of reaction.

Round and round the android's shell-hard green ankles the Empts scurried. *Chee-wee!* Suddenly the ball tip of the laser beam dipped.

Blecho let the weapon drop at a careless angle. The ruby beam played over the plasto surface of the egg, crazing it instantly. The android's head lolled. The Empts had him!

Three Empts frolicked near Barton Lummus now. His chins shook as he chuckled. All at once his face went slack except for that moon grin.

Lummus sat down, legs spread, looking exactly like an oversized child at play.

One of the Empts hopped upon Lummus' left leg, regarded him with its faceted hollow eyes. Lummus giggled. With elaborate gentleness, he patted the Empt's armor.

"Amusing. Ah, yes. Amusing indeed."

Rob waited till he was sure both Lummus and Blecho were completely under the power of the Empts. The android paid no attention to the destruction his laser beam was causing to the surface of the egg. Lummus bobbed his melon head and crooned nonsense syllables at the three creatures near him. Rob visually gauged his course down the slope—a wide loop to the left, to stay out of the way of the Empts. He jumped up and plunged down into the depression on the run.

Blecho heard him first. The emerald head rotated toward him, but Blecho took no other action. Barton Lummus saw Rob speed by and continued to grin in a bemused way. His lenslike brown eyes had difficulty focusing.

Lyndsey was the only one who recognized him. She cried out his name as he dropped to his knees, struggled to unfasten the belt around her wrists and ankles.

"I thought I'd never see you or anyone again," Lyndsey said in a ragged voice.

"As soon as I get this off, we'll get out of here."

Lyndsey's blue eyes darted past his shoulder, fearful. "That awful man! He's *giggling*."

"Footloose rounded up the Empts for me."

"Footloose!"

"I came across him at the Phylex Station. I took a chance that the Empts would make Lummus and his green pal forget who I was. Obviously I'm not a pleasant memory to that fat crook. Looks like the trick worked, too. Just a second more, Lyndsey—"

Rob's hands were slippery, and the belt had been securely knotted. He bit at the last knot with his teeth, loosening it. He broke a fingernail trying to wiggle his finger into the crack between the strands of the knot. At last he forced his finger through.

He tugged hard. The knot came loose. The belt dropped off.

Rob slipped his right hand around Lyndsey's shoulder. He stood up slowly, drawing her with him. All at once her knees gave out. He supported her for a second as she wobbled.

"Lean on me and walk," Rob whispered with a glance at

Lummus. The fat man was still crooning to the Empts in a wordless monotone.

Lyndsey's breathing was strident, uneven. She was a heavy weight against Rob's shoulder as they started up the ridge. With a loud crack the surface of the plasto egg gave way. Oblivious, Blecho continued to play the laser beam into the interior of the power station. Purple sparks crackled. Smoke fumed.

Half running, half walking, Rob and Lyndsey hurried up the slope, while the Empts kept Lummus and the android busy. All at once, though, Rob became conscious of a peculiar sound.

It came from the sky. A low, steady chuttering. The moon of Stardeep, huge as a small planet, was just looming up over the mountains. It shed a bilious green light that reflected on five specks approaching in the sky from the direction of the Phylex Station.

Rob shielded his eyes. The chuttering grew louder. Abruptly he recognized it. "Those are flyers! The Conpats, I'll bet." He wanted to cheer.

The five specks came on at remarkable speed. They dropped to skim the foothills, took on definition. They were teardrop shaped, with landing skids below. The sputter of thrusters became a roar as the flyers swept on toward the depression. They were the most welcome sight in the world.

An Empt let out a high-pitched *chee-wee*. Rob looked back. His stomach flipflopped.

The Empts were fleeing.

They extended and retracted pseudopods wildly as they scattered up into the rocks around the depression. The sound of the flyers had terrified them.

The last two Empts scampered out of sight. Blecho shook his head, switched off his laser beam. Barton Lummus staggered to his feet. His eyes were no longer bemused. From deep in his throat came a pebbly growl of rage.

"Blecho?" he howled, pointing. "Catch them, Blecho!"

Rob dragged Lyndsey toward the ridgetop. "Run for it!"

The android was remarkably fast now that he had returned to his senses. He sped up the slope past Lummus. The fat man reached out, grabbed the laser beam. Blecho ran on without breaking stride.

Lyndsey was stumbling again. Rob's feet were raw with pain. The dash up the slope had reopened some of the cuts that had clotted earlier. His left sandal was slippery with fresh blood. He heard Blecho churning the pumice close behind and pushed Lyndsey ahead of him to keep her out of the android's reach. Suddenly his foot twisted inside the bloody sandal. He slipped to one side.

He struggled to right himself, couldn't. He hit the pumice in a sprawl.

The android loomed against the darkening sky of Stardeep, emerald cheeks reflecting the green beams of the huge moon. Blecho's blank eyes shone as he groped for Rob's throat with both hands.

Rob picked up a chunk of pumice, tossed it with all his strength. The android ducked. The chunk sailed on down the slope and struck Lummus on the head.

The fat man let out a cry of rage, his melon head shaking, his small beard jiggling. He whipped the laser beam up to fire—

Blecho almost had Rob's neck. Somehow Rob got his footing, started away. Lyndsey cried a warning about the laser beam.

"Out of the way, Blecho!" cried Lummus. The android doubled at the waist.

This gave Lummus a clear target—Rob struggling up the slope.

Lummus aimed the laser beam. Rob jumped to one side just the instant Blecho stood up. He had a wicked piece of pumice clutched in one emerald hand.

The android hadn't heard his master. Blecho flung the rock as Lummus discharged the beam.

There was a blaze of red light, an aftercrackle, a horrible, rasping cry.

Rob's vision blurred as the pumice hit, a corner of it skating across his eye. All at once the left side of his face was warm and wet. The pumice-chunk had opened a wound at the corner of his eye.

Rob lurched toward a small boulder, tumbled against it. Everything revolved at dizzying speed. The roar of the flyer thrusters became a din. Rob shook his head from side to side. His left eye was totally useless.

A Conpat flyer was landing near the power station. Its ground-effect skids blew up clouds of dust. The whole scene crawled with weird shadows—or perhaps that was only in Rob's mind.

Men jumped out of the flyer. Lean men in black boots. Another flyer came down right behind.

There was another cry from along the slope to the left. Dimly Rob knew he had to respond to it.

He shoved himself away from the small rock with both hands. He staggered a few steps, hit his bloodied foot against something slippery-hard, glanced down. A sour choking constricted his throat.

Nothing remained of Blecho the android except a charred strip of cloak and two emerald feet with toes upturned to the moon. Somewhere down in a glassy mass of fused pumice, a blank gray eye seemed to glimmer—

Lyndsey screamed Rob's name.

Shambling, Rob moved toward the crest of the ridge. The girl was struggling with a misshapen, melon-headed thing made out of shadow. The immense moon of Stardeep was right behind them like a giant illuminated screen. The glare blinded him.

The shadow-thing—Lummus!—reached arms around Lyndsey's middle. The fat man lifted her bodily, carried her out of sight down the other side of the ridge.

Rob staggered on. In the depression, all the Conpat flyers had landed. Rob thought he heard Simon Ling's voice bawling orders. Spotbeams rose up through iris ports on the tops of the flyers, began to whirl spears of white light in circles.

The beams flicked across Rob's back as he fought toward the top of the slope. Each time a beam passed over him, it threw his silhouette ahead on the ground. The chaos of lights, shouting, his own pain, became a nightmare . . .

He was aware of cool wind on his bloody cheek. The top of the ridge. He was in the open, dwarfed by the gigantic green-tinged moon. Out in the darkness of the foothills, a little red eye blinked. Somehow Rob knew enough to fall to the side.

The laser beam gouged a trough where he had been. The aftercrackle died. The pumice bubbled and fused into a glasslike glob.

"Young master—the rest of you—" The strangled voice was far away. "I have the girl—and I have a map of the mountain caves—"

Men pounded up the slope behind Rob, thrust around him. He recognized Simon Ling's huge frame, his hooked nose. *Flick-flash* went the revolving beams from the flyers.

"Down!" Simon shouted, knocking two of his men aside as the red eye winked.

The blast missed. More men were spilling to the top.

"Here's the portabeam, Commander."

"Keep that thing off!" Simon snarled. "It just makes us better targets." His voice broke. "That—that lunatic's got Lyndsey."

Rob was on his hands and knees. He felt warm, drowsy, unable to think with coherence. *Flick-flash*. His shadow chased across the pumice in front of him. And before the beam swept on, he saw blood fall from the blinding wound beside his eye and spatter like a red flower on the ground. *Flick-flash*.

"Lummus?" Simon Ling shouted. "Don't hurt the girl!"

"Then don't you come after me!" came the faint, wind-blown voice. "I'm going for the caves. If you so much as set foot—"

The wind shattered the rest. A hand touched Rob's shoulder.

"The boy's hurt, Commander."

Simon Ling said something Rob didn't understand. His wrists were turning to jelly. He couldn't even prop himself up any longer.

Rob keeled over on his side, unconscious.

# Fourteen

## FOOTLOOSE AFRAID

"How long have I been out?" Rob wanted to know.

Simon Ling was stalking back and forth in front of him like a caged animal. There were pits of shadow beneath his eyes.

"About an hour," the Commander answered.

One of the flyer spotbeams had been adjusted downward to illuminate the area around the power station. There were at least fifteen Conpats present. Most carried sidearms. One approached holding a small plio-covered bar of some dark stuff.

"I broke this out of one of the field kits, Commander."

"Thanks, Gerrold. Want something to eat, Rob?"

"Yes!" Rob was a little startled at the intensity of his response.

He unwrapped the bar, bit into it. Synthetic. But its strong beef flavor made it taste magnificent.

As he chewed he discovered that his left cheek hardly hurt at all. He paused long enough to run a finger up past his left eye. Alongside it he felt a springy, slippery patch where skin should be.

Simon Ling didn't notice. He was staring out past the brilliant light to where the moon of Stardecp was just discernible as a greenish ball. The Conpat named Gerrold told Rob: "We dressed those cuts with aerosols from the medikits. That wound was the worst. What you feel on your cheek is an osmosis stitch. The plasto resin will grow the edges together and be absorbed through your pores in about three hours. Does it hurt much?"

Rob shook his head. His feet, particularly the left one,

were completely free of pain too. He wolfed more of the beef bar. Then:

"Commander?"

"Yes?"

"What about Lyndsey? I tried to stop Lummus—"

"I know you did," Simon said in a bleak voice. "I'm grateful. But I can't make a move in that direction till we get the poacher ship squared away."

"How do you know about that?"

"It got to be pretty obvious by the time we got here, Rob. There's always a ship. There has to be, to transport the Empts off Stardeep. We picked up the distress beacon back in Churchill this afternoon—"

"I triggered that in the flyer," Rob nodded.

"Right. The beacon set off coordinating signals from the nearest Phylex Station. We knew the source of the call immediately. I sent a crew to the yard for a flyer. They talked to the mech on duty. He reported that three other people had gone out with you this morning. I discovered one of them was Lyndsey. I checked our domidome. She was gone, all right. So I came out with my men. Just as we approached the Phylex antenna, we began to pick other signals up indicating power station malfunction. Those installations don't burn out of their own accord. The failsafes are too elaborate. So that meant one thing—poachers, with their ship waiting upstairs for the barrier to break. What about you?"

As quickly and clearly as he could, Rob described all the events after Barton Lummus stopped him outside the hostel that morning. Commander Ling listened without comment. He stood with his thumbs hooked on his black belt, his profile sharp against the glare of the spotbeam.

Rob described the trip overland to the power station. He told how he had used the Empts supplied by Footlóose to lull Lummus and the android while he rescued Lyndsey.

"That was pretty fair thinking." Simon meant it as a compliment.

"Only it didn't work. Commander"—Rob strained to sit up, moving from the flyer skid where he had been leaning—"we've got to get her away from that man!"

"I know, Rob. It's"—a fraction's hesitation—"just as heavy on my mind as it is on yours. More."

Somewhere a communicator began to beep. A Conpat ran up.

"We just got word, Commander. They've located the poacher ship."

An almost icy smile etched Simon's wide mouth. "Is she secure?"

"She is, Commander. Boarded and secure, with all hands prisoner. She was right where we thought she'd be. *Moonlet Hopper* is her name. A registry cert from Johnson's Third. The captain—Ridirigo, or something like that—folded his flag immediately. No one was hurt."

Simon gave a sharp nod. "All right. Now let's worry about my daughter."

The Conpat who had provided the beef bar said, "We're breaking out search gear, sir."

"No!"

Rob was taken aback by Simon's intensity. Even the Commander himself was a little embarrassed. He continued with forced calm. "No, don't do that. I want to go in after her with a very small party. That's the only safe way. Too many men and Lummus will know he's being chased. We need surprise working for us, especially in the caves." Simon twisted around. "Where's the man with the beard?"

"Wandering around here somewhere," Gerrold answered.

"Get him."

Soon two of the Conpats returned with Footloose shambling between them. The Conpats already looked faintly glaze-eyed. They backed off to a safe distance and recovered their alertness.

Standing near Simon Ling, Rob felt a faint tingling playing at the front of his skull. He took a step to the rear, another. All at once he remembered his father, *Majestica,* the reasons he had come to Stardeep. But he didn't need the momentary memory lapse caused by Empting to erase those memories. The events of the day were doing a very effective job of frustrating his original plans. He felt a quick, sudden pang of defeat.

Simon was speaking.

"Footloose? Do you know who I am? Don't you remember me from Churchill?"

The man's blue-chip eyes glowed in the spotbeam. His chained Empt nestled against one leg, going *chee-wee* softly.

"Conpat Commander person, you," Footloose replied. Evidently the memory wasn't unpleasant.

"Please listen carefully. The man who took my daughter—"

Footloose shook his head. He smiled that strange, wistful smile to show he had forgotten. But Simon kept right on. ". . . still has her. In the caves, I think. I've been in some of the Stardeep caves many times, but not the ones in this area. Have you been in these caves?"

Footloose surprised everyone by fisting the hand to which the chain of his Empt was attached.

"Don't ask, you Commander person! Don't ask!"

"Footloose, my daughter's life depends on this. Do you know the caves?"

"Don't want to go in there!" Footloose exclaimed. "Won't go there, that place." And he spun, starting to run off.

Three wiry Conpats barred his path. Suddenly Footloose bent down. He pulled his Empt into the crook of his arm. He pressed his cheek against the creature, hiding his mouth against the little beast's armor while he made unintelligible sounds. The Conpat named Gerrold strode to Simon's side. His voice was low.

"He's terrified, Commander."

"Of something strong enough to counteract even Empt energy," Simon agreed.

"That would have to be pretty strong," Gerrold breathed.

"Footloose?" Simon began again. "What do you remember about the caves that makes you afraid to go there?"

The Empt let out a sharp *chee-wee* as Footloose hugged it fiercely. The bearded man was breathing in noisy gulps. Suddenly Rob noticed that there were tears in the corners of the young-old eyes.

"Don't make me, Commander person," Footloose whispered.

"I need a guide, Footloose."

"But—" The bearded man shook his head violently. "Can't. *Can't.*"

Astounded, Rob wondered what powerful memory or emotion could be tearing at the man's dazed mind with enough force to nullify the Empting process. Simon stepped one pace closer. He lowered his voice, spoke swiftly, convincingly.

He reminded Footloose almost the way Rob had done that he, the Commander, had helped Footloose recapture his runaway Empt in Churchill. "And who sent a flyer over the barrier every time you wanted to come into town for what you call your victuals? I did! Commander Ling! I wouldn't ask this of you, but a criminal called Lummus took my daughter as a hostage."

Footloose dragged a perspiring hand across his brow. "All cloudy, person. Something wrong. Did this once already."

"Yes," Simon emphasized, "you did. You tried your best, and so did the young man you helped. The two of you tried to get Lyndsey back. Through no fault of yours, Lummus got her again."

Footloose located Rob in the glare, pointed. "Edison person. He was the one." The man's bright-blue eyes still gleamed with unexplained tears.

"We have to make another try, Footloose. Another one, understand?"

Simon spoke with patience and quiet force. Rob knew that he must be torn with worry, but somehow he kept it almost completely hidden.

"I'm going into those caves myself, Footloose. But I really need an expert to show me the way. Have you been in the caves around here? Give me a straight-out answer."

Footloose clutched his Empt. "Commander person, please not—"

"Answer me!"

"The caves I know. Many times—too many times. But—don't want to go."

"Why not? Your Empt will keep you from being afraid."

"Not from everything," Footloose sobbed. "Not from—from—"

A dazed headshake. Then silence.

"What's in the caves that you fear, Footloose?"

The bearded man simply wouldn't answer. He hugged his squealing Empt and hid his face.

Gerrold and the other Conpats watched their Commander. Simon Ling chewed on his lower lip. He waited.

Finally, struggling against awful emotion, Footloose raised his head. His eyes were haunted. His voice was barely audible.

"Commander person, I—remember good things of you. I don't—want to go. But—for you I—I—"

He turned his back, shuddering. A moment later Rob and the others heard the whispered word. "Yes."

"Thank you," Simon sighed. "We'll move out right away. Gerrold? I want a homing device."

In another moment the Conpat brought one. Simon Ling clipped the small black box onto his belt. He adjusted the controls.

"Set up flyer four as the monitor. See if you're reading."

Another of the Conpats rushed away, climbed up inside a flyer. There was a burst of static, then a sustained warbling tone.

"O.K.," Simon called. "Keep tight on my signal so you can come into the caves right away if I program the distress tone. Now let's see. I'll need a sidearm, a tracker, a torch, some rations—"

While the Commander's men ran to fetch the supplies, Footloose was huddled against one of the flyers, still hugging his Empt to his chest. Rob walked over to Simon.

"I'd like to come along, Commander."

Simon smiled, without humor. "I would have been surprised if you hadn't asked, Rob. I think you've earned it. Just the three of us, then. You and I and our frightened guide." With unhappy eyes Simon studied the bearded man's trembling back. "I hope he can stay coherent long enough to help us find my girl."

# Fifteen

## INTO THE CAVES

In less than half an hour all the Conpat flyers but one took off. The green moon, an immense shadow-pocked ball in the sky, made the disappearing craft glitter and wink as they sped away over the waste toward Churchill.

Inside flyer four, Commander Ling was checking final details with the two Conpats who had stayed behind to monitor his homing device. Rob sat on the ground outside, gnawing another bar of synthetic beef. His mouth and eyelids felt gritty—the former because of his exposure to the constant wind, the latter because he was exhausted. He knew he wouldn't get a chance to sleep for many hours yet.

Boots rattled in the pumice. Rob ate the last of the bar, got up.

"All set, Commander?"

Simon didn't miss the signs of weariness. "Are you sure you want to come along, Rob?"

"Yes, sir. I have to go."

Simon gave one crisp nod, cupped hand to his mouth. "Footloose?"

The bearded wanderer shambled into the light circle cast by the spotbeam. His eyes were hidden beneath the brim of his battered hat. At least he's stopped crying, Rob thought. His Empt was docile, at the end of the alloy chain.

"I'll go first until we reach the caves," Simon advised them. "We'll follow the tracks with this." He waggled the plasto cylinder strapped to the inside of his right wrist.

The cylinder's pointed end emitted a faint beam of purplish light. Rob had difficulty seeing it clearly. "This is the tracker," Simon explained. "Unfortunately it's only good

for a few hours. Then a special sensor cell has to be replaced. We'll have to move as fast as we can. Come on, I'll
show you."

The Commander started for the crest of the ridge. Rob
followed. The Empt went, *Chee-wee*. Footloose responded
with two similar sharp cries. At a safe distance, he started
after the others.

They climbed the ridge and went down the other side to
the bottom. There Simon stopped. A sizable boulder cast a
thick shadow across the open area. Where the pumice
glowed under the direct moonlight, Rob detected shallow
indentations. The indentations led toward the shadow
thrown by the rock.

Commander Ling adjusted dials on the wrist cylinder.
"A tracker is sensitive to human tissue. What was Lummus
wearing on his feet?"

"Boots, I think," Rob said.

Simon played the cylinder's feeble light into the rock's
shadow. A pattern became visible, like a scattering of lumi-
nous purple dust.

"Then that footprint belongs to Lyndsey. It's too small
for Lummus, anyway. Let's see—yes, I remember. She put
on sandals this morning. You see, Rob, the tracker works
because human dermal tissue constantly sloughs off in mi-
croscopic bits. The tracker's sensitive to the deposits even
in total darkness."

He raised the beam. A foot or so ahead, where the land
sloped upward again, another eerie purple cluster glowed.
By a trick of his tired eyes, Rob imagined a great purple
nebula whirling in space.

"Let's go," said Simon.

In silence they followed the glowing skin-prints for
nearly ten minutes. Behind them Footloose scrambled
along, chain clinking. The young-old man muttered to himself. Though his hysterical mood had passed, he obviously
wasn't happy.

The three of them moved in and out of splashes of pale-
green moonlight. Twice they lost the trail, had to double
back to the last scatter of purple motes that seemed to float
in the shadows before them. Each time they located the
right way to go by finding the patch of purple dust they
had missed earlier.

But each delay cost them time. Before Rob realized it,

the moon was setting. He mentioned this to Simon, who nodded.

"We'll have about two hours of total darkness before false dawn. That's when the tracker really becomes useful. I just hope the sensor cell lasts that long."

"Lummus could duck into the caves almost anywhere, couldn't he? I've seen what looked like two entrances already."

"Yes, he could. But he hasn't so far."

"He does have a map," Rob reminded the Commander.

"I'll wager it's an old copy of one prepared by the first geol team on Stardeep. Tourists get them in gray markets along with phony sales deeds for the mineral wealth just waiting to be picked up in the caverns. When the tourists reach one of the barriers, they discover they've been fleeced. Besides, there isn't any mineral wealth underground. Just vast networks of caves, big ones and small. Interconnecting, it's said, for thousands of miles under the surface."

"And that's where the Empts live?"

"Not quite. They spend most of their time in the open. The females go into the big rooms underground to lay their eggs and hatch their young. A female Empt will stay with her babies for about two weeks. Then she leaves them. About a week later the babies mature. It's a short life cycle. Empts live about four years. All during that time"— Simon's voice hardened—"they're prey for snakes like Lummus. We—oh-oh. Go left, Rob."

Their passage up through the foothills became increasingly difficult once the moon was down. They stumbled often, blundered into boulders, required a longer and longer time to locate a purplish patch and search out the next one. Either Rob's tiredness was catching up with him or the air was growing thinner. He had trouble breathing again.

At one point Footloose cried out from behind them: "High enough, Commander person. We turn back."

"No, Footloose," Simon said flatly.

"Bad things here. Too dark. Too many voices talk-talk in the dark."

Simon swung around. "You mean you heard something?"

"Little voices, person. I hear. *I* hear. Not you."

"What's he afraid of?" Rob whispered.

"Can't imagine," Simon returned. "The poor devil. The

way he's mumbling to himself, we may wind up going into the caves without any guide at all."

"Need to go back," came the sad, unsteady voice. "Go back."

After fifteen minutes of searching for the next telltale patch, the Conpat commander called a halt. They sat down to rest.

"We're losing time, not gaining it, crashing around this way. And the tracker's cell is almost done for. We'll go faster when it's light. Let's wait till false dawn.

"But Lummus might—" Rob began. He stopped, regretting that he had said even that much.

Simon adjusted the lens on the tracker. The purple beam looked feeble as it modulated to a pale blue, lighting the rocky nook into which they had stumbled. The Commander sank down with his back against a stone. Despite the coolness of the predawn air, sweat streaked his cheeks. His eyes were circled with shadows.

"I don't think he'll harm her," Simon said, though without a great deal of conviction. "I think he's bluffing us. Poachers are the low rung on the criminal ladder. Vicious only up to a point. Lummus won't want a homicide to his credit."

"He said as much when we landed at the Phylex Station," Rob remembered. But he wasn't convinced.

Simon glanced at him uneasily. The Commander was plainly worried about the wait. Still, it was the only practical thing to do.

Rob leaned his forehead against a cool stone. Footloose came clattering into the patch of bluish light. Rob watched him through half-closed lids. He kept up a constant mumbling monologue. His hat was pulled far down over his eyes, as if to avoid the glances of the others. Tiny beads of perspiration glistened in his straggly beard.

At long last, a thin sliver of lemon light appeared along the faraway horizon.

"Time." Simon heaved to his feet.

As their surroundings became visible, they had less trouble maneuvering between the jutting boulders. They had left the pumice behind and now clambered upward over smooth slatelike surfaces. Simon intensified the pace as the light increased.

For a man of his bulk, he was very quick, squeezing through narrow places and pulling himself up short, sheer vertical surfaces with apparent ease. Rob had to push to keep up. And the higher they climbed, the grimmer Simon looked.

Presently visual tracking of the runaway and his victim became easy—they spotted a scuff mark on a ledge, a patch of small stones disturbed. The purple peaks loomed above them in the light. As they inched along a ledge with the warming breeze gusting around their legs, Rob glanced down and sucked in his breath.

He hadn't realized how far they had come. The boulder-strewn slope fell away a good mile below them. The power station egg gleamed down there like a cracked toy.

Footloose was noisier than ever. He talked exclusively to himself. The tone was that of an utterly terrified man.

They passed the round entrance to a cave. Footloose moved out to the edge of the ledge, dragging his Empt with him. The Empt wanted to dart into the black hole. Footloose gave a savage tug on the chain. The Empt squealed.

Footloose's face had grown ugly. White teeth glared between peeled-back lips. Rob remembered seeing that ferocious expression in Churchill. It was a terrifying thing to behold.

Ahead, the ledge curved around the rock face. Simon was busy directing the all-but-invisible purple beam on the ledge itself. He missed the sudden flurry of color that Rob saw out past the turning of the ledge.

Straw-colored hair glowed in the risen sun. A melon head jiggled and bobbed. Brown lens eyes stared across an intervening declevity, then were gone.

"I saw them, Commander!"

Simon's head snapped up. "Where?"

Rob pointed. "That cave. I'm sure I saw Lyndsey and Lummus go in there."

"Did Lummus see you?"

"I think he did. I'm not sure."

"Hury it up, Footloose," Simon called. "This is where we need you. We're going in that cave across the ravine."

As if the Commander had set off a triggering device, Footloose reacted immediately. He planted his horn-hard bare feet on the ledge, wrapped the Empt chain around his wrist, began to shake his head from side to side. His blue-chip eyes beneath the brim of his hat were pricked with the sun's highlights.

"No, Commander person. Hear many little voices now. Can't go."

Tension exploded in Simon's voice. "I helped you, Footloose. Now you're going to help me."

"No, Commander person. No, no!"

*"Keep your voice down!"* Simon's whisper still managed to be a roar. "Look at me!"

Slowly the bearded man raised his head. Tears streaked his cheeks again.

"I wish not. Oh, I wish not."

"Tell me what frightens you, man!"

The wet blue eyes blinked open. "Much, person. The little voices and—much."

"But we're going."

At last, with a gulping sob, Footloose signified his acceptance of the Commander's orders. He bowed his head and started to shuffle forward along the ledge. Simon glanced at Rob—helpless, mystified, not a little angry. He made a sharp, sudden sign to resume the march.

It took them twenty minutes to negotiate the shallow ravine separating this ledge from the one on to which the cave opened. They went down hand over hand, climbed back up the same laborious way. Simon pulled Rob up with one powerful hand. When he clenched his mouth against the Empt power and leaned down to offer the same assistance to Footloose, the bearded man waved him away angrily. The Empt rode on Footloose's shoulders as its master climbed.

At last Footloose was beside them. Simon unsnapped the holster of the sidearm he had put on at the power station—a laser beam, Rob saw. With a last glance at the lemon sun hanging over the waste, he ducked into the cave mouth and flattened against the wall. Rob was next. Footloose came last, making an inordinate amount of noise. The Empt's faceted eyes looked like molten coins in the gloom.

Here the air was sweet, cool and damp. Ahead, Rob saw nothing but a faintly moist rocky floor slanting downward to complete darkness.

Footloose started muttering again. Simon glared. It did no good. He drew the laser beam cautiously up in front of his chest. His head bobbed. He moved out. Rob followed.

They moved downward for about a dozen feet. The damp darkness closed in. Footing was uncertain. Simultaneously, the rattle of a rock echoed far ahead, and Simon hissed a warning. A red eye blinked.

The red beam carved a thin, smoking channel from the cave wall directly above Rob's head. The ozone smell and the aftercrackle were intensified by the confined space. Footloose yelped. Simon dove on his face and so did Rob.

The laser beam spurted again. It touched the Empt skittering on the end of his chain. There was an awful squeal, a puff, a reek like smoldering leather—

The end of the chain swung free. The last link was sheared in half. The link fell off. It dropped into the steaming puddle that had been the little Empt.

"Told you, person!" Footloose howled. His hat had gotten knocked off. His blue eyes were wild.

He blinked several times, shook his head violently. He glanced down at the puddle. Grief made him shudder.

"Didn't I tell you, Commander?" Footloose boomed. His voice was unexpectedly free of all slurring. "I told you we shouldn't go on, and we won't. You won't force me this time!"

Rob thought he heard noise far down the tunnel, scrambled up, turned that way. He heard Footloose move, whipped his head around as Simon rolled onto his back to defend himself.

Footloose held a rock in one hand. He ducked in, churned his arm in a big arc. The rock struck Simon's left jawbone.

Simon shuddered, made a choking sound. His head fell back. His mouth dropped open. His eyes were glazed.

Footloose turned to Rob. He advanced in a tense half crouch. The blue chips of his eyes burned.

"You won't force me into the caves either," he said.

Rock raised, Footloose sprang.

# Sixteen

## THE METAL ROOMS

Rob leaped back. His sandal slipped on the moist floor. He caromed against the wall, ducked his head as Footloose brought his arm down.

The blow missed Rob's ear by inches. The rock scraped a gouge in the tunnel wall.

The light was uncertain. Only a feeble lemon glow penetrated this far into the tunnel. Maneuvering was difficult.

Rob darted under Footloose's arm. Simon was struggling to sit up, knuckling his eyes. All at once, as Footloose turned and shambled after Rob, the Conpat Commander grasped the situation. He came to life instantly, rolled onto his stomach, shot out his hands.

Simon caught Footloose in mid-stride, just as he swung the rock again. Rob bent backward from the waist. His head hit the other wall of the cave. Simon's hard pull on the bearded man's ankle was enough to shorten the range of the swing. The rock whizzed by Rob's forehead.

On his knees, Simon grappled his arms around Footloose's legs. "Help me get the rock!" he yelled.

In two strides Rob had his fingers on Footloose's wrist. He levered it back and forth. Footloose spat and snarled and swiped at Rob's head with his fisted free hand. One blow connected with Rob's neck. He gasped in pain.

Footloose hit him in the temple. But Rob refused to give up his hold. With a groan, Footloose opened his hand. The rock dropped.

Instantly Simon let go. He leaped to his feet, punched Footloose in the midsection.

The bearded man doubled at the waist. As Footloose

started to collapse, the Commander jabbed his index finger into the tangled hair directly behind the man's grimy ear.

Footloose sighed like a punctured weather balloon. He slid out on his back, eyes closed.

"There's blood on your jaw," Rob panted. His chest hurt from exertion.

"Probably looks worse than it is." Simon wiped his arm over the superficial wound. He rubbed his forearm dry on his black blouse and gazed down at Footloose unhappily. "I hated to maul him that way. No choice, though. He was really after us."

"The death of his Empt must have done it."

A quick nod of agreement. "Did you notice something odd just before he hit me?"

"What?"

"All at once his speech was coherent. More so than I've ever heard it."

"That's right," Rob remembered. "He yelled a couple of sentences that sounded as if they came from an entirely different person.

"Curious." Bleak-faced, Simon shrugged. He knelt down, examined Footloose quickly. "He isn't badly hurt. That nerve chop should keep him sleeping for about half an hour. We'll leave him here."

"Can we go on without a guide?"

"No guide at all is better than one who keeps attacking us. Besides—" Simon rose. His face stood out briefly in the wan light from the cave mouth. He looked savage. "I want to find Lyndscy."

Thinking of Lummus somewhere ahead, Rob shivered. But he said nothing as he fell in behind the Commander.

Before they had taken more than two dozen steps along the sloping rock floor, Simon put away his tracker. Its sensor cell was dead. He unhooked his tiny torch from his belt. He switched it on. The beam was thin, intense. Simon modulated the controls so that the beam diffused, becoming much dimmer at the same time. With its aid they could see more of the way ahead, but less clearly. They kept moving.

They made a turning. Rob glanced back. No light whatever showed behind them.

As they crept along, they stumbled over occasional piles of loose rock. Rob wondered where they came from. Every ten paces or so, Simon stopped to listen for Lummus. The air became sweeter and damper. Unpleasantly so. Rob's skin felt as if it were covered by a thin coating of grease.

The tunnel angled downward more steeply. They made several more sharp turnings. They had been moving for only about ten minutes, but it seemed far, far longer.

All at once Simon growled, "Hold up. There's something ahead."

Rob edged up closer. Simon ran the beam over what appeared to be an obstruction completely blocking their way. He blinked.

His eyes weren't deceiving him, nor was the feeble light. The barrier did have a matte gray appearance, except where it was stained with patches of flaky reddish-brown material. The weak beam picked out an oddly familiar oval outline in the center of the obstruction.

The Commander advanced cautiously. He rapped his knuckles on the barrier. It rang like a bell.

"A metal wall *underground?*" Simon whispered.

"With a doorway in it, too," Rob exclaimed, pointing to the oval.

He reached out, scraped his fingertips across the faintly convex barrier. His hand came away with the flaky red-brown material caked under the nails.

"And rust. Rust all over it."

"What the devil could it be?" Simon wondered. "Some kind of research facility buried down here?"

"Wouldn't the Conpats know about something like that?"

"Of course they would, unless it's been here for more than a hundred years. But that can't be. The metal shows too few signs of corrosion. Get back against the wall in case Lummus is close by. I'm going to see what's on the other side of that opening."

Rob obeyed orders. The moment his shoulders touched the tunnel wall, a portion of it gave way. He leaped across the tunnel as a mound of stones crashed at his feet.

Gradually the clatter died away. The last chunk dropped from the wall, hit the side of the pile, rattled to the bottom.

Frowning, Simon shone the beam across the section from which the rock had crumbled.

"Fragile stuff. We'd better be careful or we'll start a real cave-in."

Rob recalled the other piles of rock through which they had walked. Simon turned the torch toward the rusty surface. He dilated the torch aperture. The beam shot through the oval opening. If it was a doorway, the door had long since fallen off. The beam revealed rusty walls forming a narrow metal corridor.

A low whistle came out between Simon Ling's teeth. "This has to be some kind of underground station. Come on."

The Commander lifted one black boot over the bottom of the oval, then the other. Rob came right behind.

Once past the barrier, Rob reached up to discover a metal ceiling. Simon reduced the intensity of the light. They crept forward ten or twelve steps.

"Another doorway," Simon whispered. "I see something—" Out went the torch.

Gingerly, Rob followed Simon across the sill of the next doorway. Beyond the sill, which was flush with the floor, he could detect weld nodes through the thin soles of his sandals. All at once the entire feel of the surroundings changed.

His fingers bumped a railing on the left. Another on the right. Without being able to see a single detail of this new place in which they found themselves, Rob knew they had left confining walls behind, were on a walkway or railed platform in a much larger chamber. There was more movement of the damp, sweet air against his cheeks, plus an eerie sense of vast space all around.

"Rob!" the Commander whispered. "Look down below."

Far down to the left, a flabby figure recognizable as Barton Lummus crouched over a slumped body with straw-colored hair.

Lummus' clothing was torn. The backwash of the tiny torch he carried in his left hand illuminated a shining swathe of grease on his cheek. The light sketched in something else too—a corner of a massive piece of machinery.

The machine resembled a giant vertical wheel with vanes on its steel spokes. A curving shield ran all around its rim. Lyndsey—the crumpled shape lay against the dusty base of this incredible and unknown machine.

"Let me reconnoiter," Simon whispered. "You wait here." Then the Commander was gone.

A faint creak of the walkway—Rob was certain they were suspended high above the floor of the huge chamber—was the only tiny sound that marked his leaving. Rob clutched the rail, stared downward. He was fairly sure that he couldn't be seen.

Besides, Lummus was occupied. He rolled up one of Lyndsey's eyelids, swore loudly. Rob's stomach tightened up.

Had Lyndsey simply fainted from fright and exhaustion? Or was it something much worse? He couldn't tell.

The obese man stood up, jammed one fist against a hip, stared in disgust at his hostage. Nervously he raked his fingers through his sleek brown hair. Rob saw no more—a touch on his elbow startled him, swung him toward Simon, who had come back silently.

With his mouth against Rob's ear, Simon whispered his discovery and what he intended to do about it. Rob nodded several times to indicate he understood. Simon faded into the dark again. Rob crept forward, inching his hands on the rail till he came to a vertical support with nothing beyond. He faced about, dropped his foot down to the first rung of the ladder Simon had found.

Holding his breath, he started the downward climb. Somewhere farther on in the blackness, Simon should be moving down a second similar ladder.

A rung beneath Rob's left sandal squeaked, then sheared in half.

Rob's body dropped. His right foot hit the next rung, slowed his fall. He gripped the ladder uprights with all the strength left in his hands. His arm muscles throbbed.

When he realized that he had caught himself, the shock flooded in on him. What about the noise? Surely Lummus must have heard the creak of the fatigued metal giving way—

A low, steady *smack-splat* drifted up to him. He screwed his head around.

In the tiny patch of light cast by the torch that he had put down on the machine base, Barton Lummus crouched beside Lyndsey. He was slapping her cheeks.

"Come, come, young mistress. Enough of this cheap dissembling. We must hurry on." Lummus' voice had an odd, echoing quality, which confirmed Rob's belief that this chamber was of great size. The poacher grew more angry when his hostage failed to respond with more than a groan. *Smack-splat.*

"I won't tolerate this sort of playacting, young mistress. Wake up, you wicked minx!"

Using the sound of Lummus' voice as his cover, Rob rushed on down to the floor of the chamber. His sandals settled on metal, disturbed dust that clouded up around his knees. The dust rose higher, made him want to cough. He clapped a hand over his nose and mouth.

The spasm passed. He waited. Other huge vaned wheel machines were arranged in a long row between where he stood and where Barton Lummus squatted. Lummus had gotten no results with his slapping. He was rocking back on his haunches and scratching his scraggly chin beard as if undecided on what to do next.

Rob peered along the aisle that ran beside the immense machines. He gauged his route of attack—

Out in the dark, there was a piercing whistle. Simon's signal!

Lummus grunted. "Uhhh?" His head swiveled. Rob launched himself into a dead run.

The poacher swung toward the pounding of Simon's boots. He jerked the laser beam from his waistband, fired. Out past the glow of Lummus' torch, Simon appeared briefly. He seemed to hurl away into the darkness as the thin red tracery ate through air where he had been. In the extreme distance the intensified light met a barrier. The aftercrackle blended with a burst of sparks from disintegrating metal.

"Take him from behind!" Simon bawled to Rob, his boots thudding again.

Rob made as much noise as possible. The clang-bang of people coming at him from both sides had the desired effect. Lummus didn't fire again. Instead, he darted out of sight, to his right—Rob's left.

Rob kept running. He kicked his way through a small mound of white, stick-like things that rattled and gave off dust. He and Simon reached Lyndsey at just about the same moment. From the cross-aisle into which Lummus had darted came a yipping cry. It dwindled suddenly. There was a faint, ugly crunching.

Then complete silence.

The Commander and Rob exchanged baffled glances. Rob snatched up the torch Lummus had left. He shone it down the cross-aisle. "There, Commander! The flooring's rotted through."

"And Lummus didn't see the hole. He fell right into it."

Simon ran to the edge of the sizable opening, snapped on his own torch. He held his laser beam ready in his other hand.

When there was no deadly discharge from below, not even the faintest murmur of sound, Simon craned his head out over the opening. He played the torch back and forth.

"Looks like sand down there. No more than fifteen or sixteen feet. I'm going after him, Rob."

Simon jumped feet first.

In a second there was another crunch, followed by another, heavier and more muffled. Rob thought he heard Simon let out a dismayed cry. He edged up to the hole on hands and knees.

"Commander?"

"Here."

Simon appeared with his torch. He held something black and crumbled in his open palm.

"I smashed the homing box, blast it. Now the flyer outside isn't receiving any signal. And the tracker's useless too."

A thrill of fear coursed through Rob. They were lost in these caverns now. Lost.

"This ground is sandy," Simon called. "Seems to be the floor of another cave. Lummus is already gone. I think I see some marks showing that he crawled away."

"What kind of place *is* this?"

"I don't know," Simon cracked back. "But first things first. See about Lyndsey."

Rob hurried back to the base of the machine. He bent over the girl. He repeated her name and rubbed her wrists. It was a hackneyed technique he had seen in a dozen dipix. But he didn't know what else to do short of imitating Lummus and slapping her cheeks.

Lyndsey's eyelids looked pale and thin as fine plasto. He shook her shoulders, called her name several times more.

The girl's eyes opened, horror-filled until she recognized him. "Rob. Oh, *Rob*."

She clasped her arms around his neck and held tight. His shoulder grew damp. She was crying.

She hugged and hugged him. At last, gulping for air, she leaned back. "Is Dad with you?"

"He's—uh—down below," Rob said for want of a better term. "Can you walk?"

With his assistance, she could. They went to the edge of the hole in the floor.

"Here she is, Commander," Rob called.

Simon Ling appeared again. "Lyndsey! Lord, girl, I'm

glad you're in one piece. You two come down here. You'll have to jump. I'll keep my light on you. Can you make it, Lyndsey?"

She nodded yes. There was something close to a wan smile on her lips now. The Commander added, "Get Lummus' torch for more light, Rob."

Rob ran back to the base of the wheel-and-vane machine. He snatched up the torch, swung around. The beam swung too, sweeping across the dust-sheathed base of the machine adjoining. Suddenly Rob skidded to a stop. He turned the torch back to what he thought he had seen.

Almost obliterated by the dust. But there it was. He swallowed hard.

He walked to the machine base.

Reached out with a shaking hand.

Scrubbed the dust away with his palm.

Stared uncomprehending at the small metal plate.

The stamped-in letters were squarish, utilitarian, for identification purposes only. The letters spelled out: FTLS *Majestica.*

# Seventeen

## REVELATION

Rob couldn't believe what he saw. His hand kept shaking, and the beam of the torch wavered across the recessed letters.

From where she was standing by the gap in the metal floor—or was it a deck?—Lyndsey called to ask whether he was all right. He said yes. He wiped his wrist across his eyes, clutched the torch tighter in his other hand, turned toward the aisle down which he had come running at Lummus.

Drifting behind him, the Commander's voice: "Rob?"

"In a moment, sir. Just let me look at something."

He shone the torch on the base of the next wheel-and-vane machine. The beam skittered across dust-coated metal. He didn't see a nameplate.

Perhaps it had been an illusion brought on by hunger, physical weariness, the tension of the chase through the caves. There was no plate on this—

Yes, there was. He had missed it on his first pass of the light. This machine, too, whatever its purpose, was marked: FTLS *Majestica*.

He was unsteady on his feet as he returned to Lyndsey. She noticed.

"Rob, you look sick."

He stared down between his sandals. He was right at the edge of the opening. He noticed something he had overlooked before. There were four separate layers of plating between the one on which he stood and the one in which the bottom of the opening had been torn.

The two inner layers were a ceramic material. The indi-

122

vidual layers had air spaces between and were braced apart by alloy beams. One such beam had been sheared when the hole was punched through all the layers. The beam's end projected about six inches into the opening, knife-like. From top to bottom layer, the plating easily measured two feet thick.

Simon wigwagged his torch from below. "What's holding you, Rob?"

The impatient voice jarred him to his senses. He took Lyndsey's elbow, guided her to the edge of the hole. He said in a hoarse voice, "Try to relax when you jump. And stay to this side. Watch that beam sticking out." He shone the torch on it.

Lyndsey gave him a bewildered, almost frightened look. Her straw-colored hair hung in disarray. She was grimy, tired, miserable—and, plainly, her condition wasn't helped any by Rob staring back at one of the immense vaned machines as though mesmerized. She pushed a lock of hair away from her left cheek. She edged to the rim of the hole. Below, a foreshortened figure with hand over his eyes and torch upraised, Simon waited.

"All right, Dad," Lyndsey called, and jumped.

The Commander darted aside. Lyndsey hit and rolled. Simon bent over her, helped her up, and drew her out of range as Rob followed.

Air swept his cheeks. Its cool, overwhelming sweetness turned his stomach, made him violently dizzy during the seconds of the fall. At the last instant he remembered to unstiffen his knees.

He hit left foot first, buckled over sideways with a sharp exhalation of breath. He flopped on his side, then scrambled up, more than a little dazed. He aimed the torch overhead. He followed its beam with his eyes, afraid of what he would see.

The Commander rushed to his side, said something Rob didn't catch.

Above, the torch picked out a huge expanse of pocked, heat-streaked gray metal. Rob moved the beam to the right, adjusted it for maximum definition. The convex surface ran on and on, well out of range of even the strongest torch setting. The same thing held true when he pointed the beam to the left. The metal stretched above him like a giant ceiling. Exactly where it ended at either side of what must be another oversized cave, he couldn't tell.

"Strangest arrangement of underground rooms I ever saw," Simon commented. "I'd almost swear it looks like—"

"The hull of a ship." Rob's voice was dull. "I think it is."

"A ship?" Lyndsey said. "Down here? That's impossible."

Rob swung around sharply. "Do you know what I found on the machines up there? Nameplates. Unless I've gone crazy—and maybe I have—that's my father's ship."

That stunned Simon Ling to silence. At last he managed to say, "An FTLS underground? How—"

"I don't know how!" Rob interrupted. "But those nameplates say *Majestica!*"

Neither father nor daughter could reply. Simon's eyes were somber, thoughtful. Rob got control of himself, apologized lamely for the outburst. Simon's voice showed the effort he was putting into remaining calm. "All right. Granted that it is a ship, let's see how large it is. Put your torch beam up above with mine, Rob."

Simon's beam angled high, struck the pocked metal. Rob focused his torch on top of Simon's. The three walked left from the overhead hole, following the long axis of the convex surface.

The sand underfoot oozed cool and damp over Rob's sandals. A gash at the base of his big toe was bleeding again. He paid no attention. Lyndsey spoke in a hushed voice.

"The more you look at it, the more it does look like a hull. Half of a hull, anyway."

"Streaked by re-entry friction," Simon added. "Pocked by micrometeorites."

Rob shot his beam ahead. "There's the end of the cave."

They stared, stunned. Like an immense half-round bar of metal, the hull seemed to have been jammed by force into the damp and glistening wall of rock above. They played their torches higher. It was too far to see clearly. The vertical rock face and the impacted metal blended together into meaningless dark.

Rob's stomach ached. *Majestica* here? Somehow rammed below the surface of Stardeep? That meant there must be two thousand corpses, or the remains thereof, in the various parts of the vessel . . .

All at once he remembered running toward Lyndsey in the chamber of the machines, kicking his way through a pile of white, sticklike things that pulverized into dust. His skin crawled.

Were those the bones of two thousand dead?

Questions flooded his mind. Out in the dark, someone screamed.

A rock whizzed by, struck Simon's shoulder, glanced off.

"Torches out!" Simon bawled, extinguishing his. "Get down!"

Rob blacked out his beam, dropped to hands and knees as the wild, senseless yelling started again.

Rob slid out prone. He heard Lyndsey breathing close by. Her father was just beyond. Another rock landed with a chunk in the sand. More rocks showered on them. One hit the back of Rob's calf.

The maniacal yells continued. They seemed to come from a different direction each time. But maybe the strange acoustics of this vast underground room were playing tricks.

More rocks clattered around them.

"I'd get the laser beam on him if I could tell where he was," Simon growled.

"He keeps moving," Rob called back.

Another burst of yelling. It was the bay of a sick or wounded animal, a vibrating cry of pain and rage.

"Is it that man—" Lyndsey began.

"Lummus? It must be," Simon answered. "He may have damaged his laser beam when he fell. They're usually pretty sturdy, but—"

Abruptly the fusilade of rocks stopped. The last screech died away, echoing in the damp air.

They lay unmoving for several minutes. Rob listened hard, but detected no sound of movement. The sandy floor of the cave tended to deaden it, he suspected.

At last Simon suggested that it might be safe to get up. They did. Lyndsey lurched against Rob, apologized. Rob's stomach growled. He felt filthy. His gashed foot hurt badly. And on top of everything, there was the terror of being buried down here with Lightcommander Edison's ship and its cargo of dead men, while in the blackness, somewhere a deranged poacher stalked them—

Or was it, Rob wondered with a shock, merely the onslaught, at last, of mental breakdown?

He couldn't believe that. Everything felt real enough, including the pain.

But Commander Ling's homing device was smashed. His tracker was useless. They were cut off from help. *Why had he ever left Dellkart IV?*

In a moment the attack of near-hysteria passed, and Rob was himself again. Weary, baffled, frightened, but himself. He heard Simon's voice.

"Let's try to corner Lummus. If he doesn't have his laser beam, we can do it without too much risk. There are three of us, one of him. I'll turn on the torch. We'll spread out in a line abreast. Get between Rob and me, Lyndsey. Rob, get your torch going."

Simon's light winked on. Rob followed suit. Lyndsey moved into position, casting a long, flickering shadow across the sand.

"Now, let's walk to the far side of the cave," Simon told them. "Scuff your feet so we can see where we've been. That way, we can cover a new stretch of ground on the way back. Sooner or later we should pick up Lummus' tracks."

They moved ahead with slow, shuffling steps. They worked their way across the cave on a line roughly parallel to the gray bulk of the FTLS hull above them.

They passed beneath the ragged hole, kept going. The widened beams of the torches created a feeble swathe of light ahead. Lyndsey was the first to spot the crumpled shape that swam into Rob's beam.

Simon and Rob charged toward it. The Commander was faster. He was on his knees turning the fallen man over while Rob was still half a dozen steps away.

Lyndsey stopped, said, "Oh, Lord," softly. She turned her back and started to cry.

Simon played his torch over the misshapen mound of flesh. The details were all too recognizable.

Shabby, spotted blouse. An oversized belly. A melon head with the sleek hair out of place. The head was oddly bent to one side. The eyelids were shut. The butt of Barton Lummus' laser beam rested in the palm of his dead hand.

Shaking his head, Simon stood up. Slowly he began to shine his torch around the area.

Rob noticed a peculiar troughlike pattern in the sand. He added his light to the Commander's. They followed the trough back to a position just a little to one side of an imaginary line coming straight down from the hole in the hull.

"He must have broken his neck when he fell." The torch in the Commander's hand ranged back along the trough. "He dragged himself as far as he could before he died."

Lyndsey buried her head against her father's chest. Simon slipped his free hand around her waist. Even Rob was moved by the awful death. In a strange, weary way, Rob felt sorry for the man.

Rob's fatigued mind belatedly registered something else. "If Lummus has been dead all this time, who attacked us?"

Simon was grim. "There's only one other person it could be. Someone who knows the caves—"

"Footloose!"

"That must be it."

"Did you bring Footloose with you in here?" Lyndsey exclaimed.

The Commander said yes, described the bearded man's abnormal behavior—his protests about entering the caves, his consuming fear of something or someone underground, how he'd gone completely berserk when Lummus lasered his Empt.

"And another strange thing," Simon concluded. "Just moments after the Empt died, Footloose began talking differently."

"More coherently," Rob agreed.

"As though he'd been living for years with his mind" —Simon groped for a word, made an emphatic gesture— "like mush, because he was surrounded by Empts, and kept at least one close by at all times. The Empts helped him forget something terrible. It was so terrible that, before he attacked, he was remembering it in spite of the Empt. We knocked him out and left him. But he could have wakened in the meantime and come down here to—"

*"I hear you."*

The three froze as the voice hissed from the darkness behind them.

"I hear you all talking about me!" A rock came sailing at them.

Rob bowled Simon out of the way. The rock missed. Another flashed at them, a third.

Simon dropped his torch, charged into the darkness. Rob followed. Simon launched into a dive. Before Rob reached him, the Commander had caught the bearded man and knocked him flat.

Simon kneeled on Footloose's chest, fist drawn back, face furious. Footloose writhed.

"Stop it, Footloose. I said stop it, or I'll break you apart!"

The threat was understood. Footloose relaxed. Simon jumped up, drew his laser beam, used his free hand to search Footloose for weapons. Then he stepped back.

"What's wrong with you, Footloose? Why the devil do you want to attack us?"

Never on a human face had Rob seen such horror. Footloose whispered, "You shouldn't have made me come back down here. Shouldn't of." Blue-chip eyes glared in the light of the torch Rob had picked up. "It all came back. I knew it would, I knew it! I couldn't help remembering even with the little"—a struggle to recall a lost word—"critter." Suddenly Footloose was crying.

Fat tears rolled down his weathered cheeks and sparkled in his long beard. "The critter got shot. You caused it, you." His tearful glance indicted both Rob and the Commander. "You killed my critter, you. *You made me remember!*"

"Remember what?"

"That." Footloose pointed at the looming hull. "My name."

Simon was puzzled. "Your name is Footloose."

Eyes like blue flames, Footloose breathed, "You made me remember the real one. Mossrose."

The torch fell out of Rob's fingers, its beam flashing crazily.

"Mossrose?" Rob repeated.

Footloose sobbed. "Yes."

"Lightadjutant Thomas Mossrose?"

"Yes. Yes! *Yes!*"

# Eighteen

## DEATH OF A LIGHTSHIP

The reverberations of the awful cry died slowly. Footloose swiped at his eyes in that vague way Rob had seen before. He took three breaths, each a little steadier than the one before.

Lyndsey stood tense beside her father, alternately watching him and Rob. There was too much confusion in Rob's mind, too much shock, for him to organize a single coherent sentence. Footloose turned away.

The Commander's voice was low and hoarse. "Stand still."

"You haven't—" Footloose gulped. "You haven't got a right—"

"Yes, we have. This boy's father commanded that ship up there."

It took Footloose a while to digest the information. But instead of surprise, his face registered a curious bitterness. He stared at Rob, and for a moment his blue-chip eyes were bright with maniacal rage. Then he returned his gaze to the Commander.

Quite unnoticed, Simon had passed his torch to his daughter. Now he held his laser beam in his right hand. The ball-tipped muzzle pointed to the ground. But its significance, its threat, temporarily banished the antagonism from the bearded man's eyes.

"Edison?" Footloose said. An unsteady nod. "Rob Edison. Yes. I—" Again the leathery face wrenched. "I don't want to remember."

"You have to," Simon cracked out. "This boy came halfway across the galaxy to find out who destroyed the ship."

The bearded man fell into a steady monotone as he repeated, "Edison. Edison. You caught my critter in Churchill, Edison. I think I heard your name there."

"I mentioned it," Simon replied. "At the dome. I told you who had saved your Empt and you got excited. I thought—"

"That I was crazy? Crazy Footloose, that's what I'm called. I know it. Well, the crazy man is the man who lets himself remember"—a glance at the looming hull—"that."

"Even at the dome, the past was fighting through the Empt barrier, wasn't it?" Simon asked.

Footloose wiped his lips. "I think so."

At last Rob was able to speak. "You were my father's second."

But he didn't actually believe it yet. How could this be the same Thomas Mossrose his father's diary had characterized as warm, friendly, bright? There was terrible pain in the man's blue-chip eyes, and hatred of every memory Rob represented.

Footloose didn't reply to the question. He merely glowered.

Simon glanced at Rob, squeezed his eyes shut for the barest part of a second. Rob caught the meaning. A bluff.

Footloose was too slow to catch the glance. He shifted his hardened feet in the damp sand, picked at his raveled sleeve in a way that reminded Rob of Barton Lummus.

Simon called Lightadjutant Mossrose by his more familiar name, speaking harshly again.

"Answer his questions, Footloose."

"I don't have to do—"

A raising of the laser beam. This was the bluff. Footloose cringed.

Simon pointed the weapon at Footloose's belly. "Answer."

Silence. Footloose looked through Rob into a past where horror stirred. Slowly he spoke. "From the first day I can remember, watching the interstellars launch from Albemarle, I wanted the service, you see. I studied for the Placements and came in just one below the minimum percentile. Just one. My uncle—I don't remember his name. Ephraim, Efrem—he was high up in service administration."

Rob started to speak. Over Footloose's shoulder Simon nodded sharply, a negative. Rob's stomach hurt. He kept quiet as Footloose went on in that clear, low voice. "You can't know how much I wanted the service. None of you can. The times were right. The first FTLS were going out over bigger distances than"—he faltered, passed his browned fingers over his eyes—"immense distances. The constellations. The nebulae. My uncle used his rank. The test tapes were partially wiped. I was accepted for training. My first command—" A supple movement of his fingers, up in the direction of the ship. "Lightcommander Edison. Duncan, he said. Call me Duncan. There I was, green. Frightened. Wanting to do the best—" Again an abrupt change in mood. Footloose glared. "Don't make me tell this."

Rob swallowed. "You have to. My father died with *Majestica*."

"Not immediately, not right—"

"But he's dead. And C.D.E. has been carried on his record ever since." There was fury creeping into Rob's voice now, controlled but still real.

It took Footloose a moment to interpret Rob's statement. "C.D.—is that error?"

"Command decision error."

Lyndsey watched Rob's grimy, haunted face. She stepped closer to her father, wrapped her fingers around his arm as a bleakness spread on Rob's features, making him look implacable and very old. He felt that way.

"Your father knew—" The beaded young-old man began.

"That you were inept." *Pay them back,* Rob thought. *Pay them all back without mercy.* "He knew there was something wrong with you, Mossrose."

"Are you certain about that?" Simon asked.

"It's in my father's diary. He said his Lightadjutant didn't know astromathematics and time theory and should have been on report." Rob's voice grew more and more caustic. "But he didn't put him on report. He thought he should, but he didn't. He decided to help him. Take a chance. Give him more responsibility." A cruel, giddy excitement filled Rob now, a sense of harrying prey, of closing in on a kill. "My father gave you that chance, didn't he?"

"He was kind—" Mossrose faltered.

"He was too kind. He took the blame." A stab at the

truth, risking all: "Who was plugged into command when you launched from Stardeep?"

"I was."

"Your first launch?"

"Y—yes."

"My father wasn't linked in a tandem setup?"

"N—no, not at first. He let me try it—alone."

"And you killed two thousand men!"

Footloose lifted his gaze and stared at Rob, stared straight at him and really saw him for the very first time. Sweat shone in the scraggly hair above and below his lips.

"I know I did," he said. "God help me, I know."

Rob's nails were curled tight into his palms. The digging brought pain. The pain ignited his smoldering anger. He took a step forward. Simon dashed in front of him.

"Easy, Rob. *You heard me!*"

Rob hesitated. The Commander's eyes were fierce above his hooked nose.

"You want the truth, Rob? Be man enough to listen to it."

"But he killed—"

"Let him tell it!"

Under control again, Rob stepped back to where he had been standing. Tears reappeared at the corners of Footloose's blue eyes. He complained once more that he should not be forced to dredge up the past.

Simon reacted with equal firmness and wrath. "Don't start that. The sooner this is over, the better it'll be for all of us. The boy wants to know about the launch. Tell him."

So Footloose began, a numbed monotone: "It was a computation error. Mine. I had difficulty with the pre-launch program I prepped for the computer. One series of equations didn't fit properly. I didn't know enough to find the error, and I didn't want to admit it to the Lightcommander. So I—I fed the equations into the computer anyway. By then I think I believed they were right. We launched perfectly. We thought we went into hyperdrive for about—I don't know, three or four milliseconds—"

"Try five," Rob breathed.

"All right, five. The Lightcommander plugged into the other chair. The FTLS was creaking, all ports blanked out. We couldn't see—"

"My father programmed the correction?"

"Yes, I think so. He started—it happened too fast—by

that time it was—too late to correct any error. We weren't in hyperspace. We were here. Underground."

"Resistance!" Simon exclaimed softly. "I don't know much about hyperdrive mechanics, but I can imagine what could happen if an FTLS re-molecularized not into hyperspace but into conventional space occupied by solid rock. The resistance would de-molecularize the ship again for an infinitesimal part of a second. And because the space was already occupied, the process would continue to completion. Matter—the ship—would simply cease to exist."

Slowly Rob lifted his head to the pocked, streaked hull. He had difficulty coping with the concept. All he could imagine was an oversimplified image of a tiny metal cylinder suddenly existing, or trying to exist simultaneously with hundreds of millions of tons of rock. In a blinding instant the cylinder would be squeezed, compressed, compacted, obliterated. But if part of the cylinder, a small portion of its mass, arrived in a place in that rock where an air space existed, then perhaps—perhaps—

Rob's head ached. He pointed overhead. "That part of the ship was left?"

Footloose nodded.

"You programmed *Majestica* into the ground of Stardeep?"

"The Lightcommander tried to correct—"

"Where was he when it happened?" Rob wanted to know.

"Right alongside me on the engineering bridge. It's at the top of that huge room up there. You—couldn't see it in the dark. We—were all knocked unconscious by the impact and—half the men left alive were—broken apart inside. I woke up hours or days later. Everybody but your father and one other crewman was dead. Your father was bleeding from his nose and ears. I don't know how it happened but—I was the only one who wasn't seriously hurt. Just a broken arm, some cuts where the command chair ripped loose from its bolts and slashed me. We—found flamecutters in the gyrobal chamber. We sliced our way through the decking, down through and out. We tried to find our way to the surface of the planet. The crewman—I don't even know his name—he died. Then your father—he could barely stand—his face was all red—all red in the light from the last torch we had—"

Rob wanted to yell at the man to stop. He couldn't. In

his mind a specter of a face, awash with blood, blended with and then separated from the fax of Lightcommander Edison he had treasured so long. His ears rang. He heard Footloose reply to some question of the Commander's.

"—yes, buried. Not far—"

"Come on, Rob," said Simon.

In a dizzying nightmare, they crossed the cave floor. Simon's torch lighted the way. The floor rose slightly. Rob's vision cleared. The torch picked out two small cairns built of stones.

"I—can't remember which is the place I buried the Lightcommander," Footloose stammered.

Rob walked forward and stood by himself. His shadow fell across the crude markers.

His light-headedness vanished. His fatigue remained, but he could think clearly again, though tears clotted his eyes. He fought back all sound, but he let the tears come.

This passed. He straightened up. It was as though a cold wind had blown over him. Somehow he had passed a marking-point and changed. For all time.

He turned around to Footloose.

"You made the mistake that sent *Majestica* down here."

"I said so, didn't I? But the Lightcommander—"

"Let you command the launch. So he made a mistake too."

Command decision error. Forever on his father's record. *Belonging* there.

And the Lightcommander's error was the greater. He had permitted his Lightadjutant to have command at a critical time, and thereby risked the lives of his entire crew. It made no difference that Duncan Edison had been trying to save one man. He had destroyed two thousand.

Rob's hunt was over. His faith, his hope, was as dead as the two human beings whose remains had rotted away under those little piles of rock.

Simon sensed the crisis. "Shouldn't we face the more immediate problem, Rob?"

Hollow-eyed, Rob looked at him. "What, sir?"

"Survival. We have to get out of here." Simon eyed the suspended hull critically. "I don't know whether we can reach that opening. Maybe we can if you get on my shoulder. If that's no go, we have to find another way. Can you lead us out of here, Footloose?"

All at once Rob was very frightened.

A queer little smile twisted the face of the bearded man. He looked like someone on the verge of hysterical laughter, or complete breakdown, or both. The expressions on his face were changing as swiftly as a summer landscape on an agriworld.

The Commander repeated his question. "Can you lead us out?"

"You think I would?" Footloose breathed. The old venom was back. "Do you really think so? I lived through this! I buried the last two left alive! Dug graves with my own hands and wandered down here till I nearly lost my mind. Then I found those little critters. They helped me forget. You made me remember it all. You killed my Empt." Footloose swung to Rob. "The Lightcommander made me kill all those men. He shouldn't have let me take over."

"Watch him," Simon whispered to his daughter and Rob.

"The critter helped me! That's why I stayed out here with nobody but the critters. I had my own till you killed it!"

"Stop it," Simon barked. "There's no sense yelling at each other. We'll all die down here if we don't find a way out."

All at once Footloose grinned. "I won't die."

"What do you mean?" Lyndsey whispered.

"You need me to show you the way. There are a hundred tunnels right around this very cave—and most of them go the wrong way!" Footloose leaned forward to giggle. "That's why I did what I did up above. Followed your tracks in the tunnel to the place where you came into the ship. I kicked and banged the tunnel till a big slide started where a little one had already been started before. The top hole in the hull is blocked. You don't think so? Climb back up through the ship the way you came. Try to get out past the rocks. Try!"

While Footloose giggled, Simon stared at him as though trying to guess whether he was bluffing. From Simon's stiff expression, Rob decided that the Commander believed the claim. Well, Rob did too. This new development only added one more defeat to a string of them.

"You won't get out without me," Footloose was chortling. "Not without me, without me!"

"Then you'll take us," Simon answered.

Footloose made a menacing gesture. "I'd sooner kill you!"

The Commander shoved his daughter around behind him, raised his laser beam. "You'll do what I say. No one else knows the right way."

"But you made me remember!" He seized his temples with both hands. "You made me *hurt.*"

"Footloose—"

"*No!*" Footloose yowled and dove for the ground.

Chaos then. Lyndsey crying out. Simon pushing her to one side. Torch beams dipping crazily. Footloose snatching up handfuls of sand and flinging them in wide arcs.

The damp, gritty stuff caught Rob and Simon in the eyes. It blinded them just long enough. Footloose yelled and charged in with both fists swinging.

# Nineteen

## NO WAY OUT

Rob reached for Footloose. The bearded man eluded him, going after the Commander. His doubled left hand caught Simon in the jaw and made him reel.

The Conpat chief aimed the laser beam, just as quickly lowered it. There was a humanity in Simon that refused to do mortal harm to a poor madman, even though the madman was attacking him.

Simon ducked a second blow. He dropped his torch accidentally. Rob lunged for it. Footloose whipped up his foot. Rob took a powerful kick under the point of his chin. He staggered, fell.

Rob's hand crawled out toward the torch. He couldn't get it. His head throbbed. He saw everything as though underwater. Footloose clamped his hands on the Commander's neck.

Lyndsey darted in, seized Footloose's sleeve. The sun-faded fabric ripped in her hands. Footloose kicked her too, a vicious blow to the ankle. Lyndsey's legs failed to support her. She tumbled away.

*Help the Commander,* Rob thought. *Get up and help him.*

But he was wobbly. As he stood, the cave floor seemed to tilt from side to side.

Footloose's lips skinned back from his white teeth. He seemed to be laughing as he choked Simon. The Commander still had his laser beam in his right hand. He inverted it. Emotionless, a curious look slid over his face. He became the professional policeman, trained for self-preservation. He bashed Footloose across the bridge of his nose with the laser beam grip.

Then he drove his left hand up between his attacker's arms, jabbed for the region near Footloose's right ear. That ended it, as it had ended the first attack.

This time, however, Simon was more cautious. He rolled the unconscious man onto his stomach. He lifted the tails of the faded shirt, yanked out the piece of fibrous plasto that served Footloose as a belt. He called for the torch at closer range. Rob picked up Simon's light, added its beam to his own, and held the two while the Commander lashed Footloose's tanned wrists together.

Glumly Simon shoved his laser beam back into his belt. "We needed him."

Rubbing her calf, Lyndsey said, "Do you think he did what he said?"

Rob answered. "Yes. I think he told the truth about Dad's ship too."

Seeing the hurt on Rob's face, Simon frowned. "You came a long way to find that kind of answer. When we get out—"

"If we get out," said Lyndsey with a shudder.

"Don't talk that way, girl. Of course we'll get out. I meant to tell Rob that we can come back with exhumation gear. Seven years isn't such a long time. There are scientific tests that can identify the men in those graves. We can find out for certain whether—"

"I don't want to open the graves, sir. I know the truth."

"Grant that Footloose—or Mossrose—wasn't making anything up. Remember that your father tried to help him, not destroy him. That counts for something."

"My father did everything he has been accused of doing. Everything I knew he couldn't do."

"What are you, boy? Some kind of judicial computer?" Stung, Rob raised his head. "Sir?"

"Your father did what he did because he felt he had to."

"I defended him, sir. Lied for him."

"Your father was a human being! Not a million-cred machine with built-in failsafes. Do you really understand what it means to be a human being? It means, among other things, being imperfect!"

A great weight had settled on Rob, a sense of events drifting from his control. Here they were, buried below the crust of Stardeep, and except for a vague academic interest in his own welfare and that of his companions, he didn't really care. He was drained.

He remembered the years on Lambeth Omega-O. He remembered the cuts on his face, the hooting of a crowd of Home boys when he fought because of, and for, his father's reputation.

He remembered his own exhilaration when he left Dellkart IV, positive that he would discover the *right* truth about the past.

All the pain, the hope, the caring—for nothing.

"Don't chain yourself to the past, Rob," Simon was pleading. "I could tell that the past was making a wreck of you the first time I heard your story. Don't let it. Don't crucify yourself because a man made a mistake."

"Two thousand dead—" Rob began.

*"All right!"* Simon's voice was thunder in the cavern. "A horrible thing! But it's over! Gone and buried! The galaxy turns. Life goes on."

"I wanted to prove he was innocent. I wanted to prove that more than anything."

"And all you proved was that he was a man like other men. That's your mistake, Rob. Judging him instead of loving him."

"That isn't true. I fought for him because I loved him."

"Don't hand me that rot. You judged him, your own father, the way the rest of the galaxy did. People judged him as a bad Lightcommander. Did that make him a bad father? A bad human being? For you it did. Because that made you less than perfect too. You haven't been trying to save your father's reputation, Rob. You've been trying to polish your own. Into what? I don't know. Something shiny and flawless like one of those robot tutors I've heard about? You'll never be half the man your father was, Rob. He tried to help Mossrose. The outcome was tragic. So you'll never try anything like that. You'll keep busy worrying about yourself all the time. You'll be afraid of living. Afraid of mistakes. Afraid of—"

*"Mistakes?"* Simon's words had flayed Rob's temper raw. "We're trapped down here. Whose mistake is that? Yours!"

*"Rob!"*

Lyndsey's cry released the anguish that had been building within him. He felt bitterly ashamed and humiliated. Quickly he attempted to make amends. "I'm sorry, Commander."

"Well, I had no right to talk to you that way, either," Simon returned. "We're all tense. But the situation isn't as hopeless as all that."

The Commander checked Footloose's bonds. The bearded man remained unconscious. When Simon straightened, he was brisk again, calm but not falsely cheerful.

"We have an ample air supply. Food and water are the critical items. We can't last too many days without them. On the other hand, we know there are ways out of here. I believe our sleeping friend probably did block the upper entrance to the ship. With you two boosting me, I might make it to check. But I think we could expend our efforts more wisely."

Simon ticked two big fingers against the crumbled remains of the tiny black box that had hung at his belt. "The homing signal isn't being sent any longer. Flyer four will know something's amiss. My Conpats will come searching for us eventually. But if they have a tough time finding their way, it may be a matter of days or even a week until they reach us. That pretty well establishes priorities. Water and food."

"But where can we find them down here?" Lyndsey asked.

"Footloose must have a cache. He comes to Churchill regularly for his victuals, remember. If we can't find the cache ourselves, we'll have to make him tell us where it is."

"I wonder," Rob mused, "how much more of anything we can force out of him."

"Very little," Simon agreed. "The point is—we have to stay alive, so we'll solve the food and water problem somehow."

"I'll say it's a problem," Lyndsey sighed in a totally hopeless voice. She scuffed her foot in the damp sand. Rob stared vacantly out past the periphery of the torch beams. His weary mind picked up a statement Simon had made, toyed with it. Finally he realized its implications.

If it took the Conpats a week or more to locate them, he would very likely miss his connections back to Dellkart IV. Therefore he would miss the start of the entrance examinations. All of Exfore's dire warnings came back: Someone else in his place in college, his own life potential drastically reduced—why, he'd have to labor until he died just to pay off the loan he had gotten to come here. Failure to return to Dellkart IV on time would simply and effectively wipe out his future. As if he really had any, now that he knew the truth about *Majestica*.

It was all too confusing and disheartening to think about.

"Let's make a start," Simon grumbled.

"How?" Lyndsey asked.

"Take torches. Head for the perimeter of the cave. Try to find tunnels. We could follow Footloose's trail and make short work of it if the tracker cell was still good."

"Come on, Rob," Lyndsey urged.

He picked up one of the torches. But he was just going through the motions. Listlessly he followed Simon's lead. Lyndsey fell in step beside him. They tramped toward the darkness that the torches pushed back little by little. Rob was hungrier than he had ever been before.

"Rob?" Lyndsey said as they walked.

"What?"

"I'm sorry Footloose told you what he did."

"It was only the truth," he returned. "People are supposed to respect the truth, aren't they?"

"All the same, I know it was an awful shock. So much has happened—you must be about to drop over."

"I'm fine."

"There's the wall," Simon called from ahead.

They used the torches to search a wide area for about twenty minutes. They found no openings. Simon directed them to the next section to the right. Once more they searched the cave walls, playing the beams up and down carefully. Once more it was the same, futile story—implacable, unbroken rock.

They searched the next section. The next. Even Simon began to sound upset. "I know for a fact there are tunnels. I've been in them on other parts of the planet!"

"There may be only one or two entrances to this cavern," Rob suggested. "And we've explored just on this side of the ship. The cavern might be bigger than we think. It could take days."

For the first time Simon's rugged face showed hopelessness. "It could. But let's keep going."

They searched for three hours more. They worked their way beneath the hull of the great lightship, out into the part of the cavern beyond. It was huge, as Rob had suggested. Again the rock walls revealed no sign of a break.

Weariness began catching up with all of them. Simon dropped his torch twice.

As they were preparing to move to another section of wall, Rob admitted to himself that they would probably have to wait for the coming of the Conpats—if the Conpats found them. He felt light-headed again. *Well,* he said to himself, *I've lost everything else. What does a chance at college matter?*

Suddenly Simon's alarmed voice broke in. "Where's Lyndsey?"

They swung the torches, crisscrossing the sand. Simon grew pale.

"I didn't see her walk off," Rob said.

"Lyndsey?" Simon sounded desperate as he shouted. "Lyn!"

*Lynlynlynlynlyn* went the echo, singing away.

From far to their right came an answer, very faint. "Dad. Over this way."

Rob heard a high-pitched sound. It seemed to come from the same general direction as Lyndsey's reply. He thought he should recognize the sound. His weary mind refused to provide the identification. And somehow the squeaking terrified him.

"Lyndsey?" He bolted into a run. "Lyndsey—we're coming!"

# Twenty

## EMPT TIMES TWO

Simon kept up with Rob as Lyndsey called out to guide them. All at once Rob saw small strange splotches of yellow in the blackness. They glowed, vanished, glowed again like gems.

The strange brilliance was located directly ahead of them now, and somewhat over their heads. The damp sand sloped upward just a little.

"I'm up here, Dad." Lyndsey sounded quite close. "In this little niche."

Her shadow passed between Rob and the yellow spots. He flogged his mind for the obvious answer and all at once he had it. The sound was repeated, *Chee-wee*. Empt eyes! Empts crying!

But why were the cries so high and thin?

As they climbed the sandy slope and Simon directed his torch into the natural recess in the rock, Rob saw the reason. Simon put words to it.

"Babies! How did you find them, Lyndsey?"

"I heard them squeaking," she explained, kneeling beside the two little creatures. Four brilliant yellow eyes were visible in the light of the torch.

One of the Empts, which was about half the size of a full-grown specimen, shot out three translucent pseudopods and tried to scuttle away into the dark. A tingling, not unpleasant, stirred at the front of Rob's skull.

Lyndsey caught the escaping creature and snuggled it against her. She laughed.

"Aren't they darlings? They must be in the last week before maturity. I don't see any sign of the mother. Dad, can we keep them for pets? Let's take them with us."

Lyndsey's eyes were bland discs in the glow of the torches. Rob marveled at her calm. It was a grotesque contrast to the disarray of her hair and her grimy appearance.

When her father didn't immediately reply, Lyndsey pleaded, "Say we can take them, Dad. Let's take them back to Churchill right this minute."

"Get back, Rob," Simon whispered. He clutched the boy's arm. "Back!"

The warning came none too soon. Rob's mind had already begun to blur. He took half a dozen sliding steps down the sandy slope. The tingling lessened.

Simon followed. In an undertone he said, "They've made her forget that we're trapped down here. She thinks everything's fine, as if all that business with Footloose never happened. As if we could just walk out of—"

Simon broke off. He turned to stare over his shoulder the way they had come.

"By heaven!"

"What's wrong, Commander?"

"For a change, nothing. Lyndsey!"

The girl was crooning to the Empt in her arms. The creature no longer seemed quite so frightened. Nor did its companion. The Empt on the ground nuzzled its plated body against her ankles. Nearby, the torch beams revealed fragments that resembled antique china overlaid with an iridescent pink. Remains of the eggs laid by the mother Empt?

"They're marvelous," Lyndsey was murmuring. "Not a bit scared of me. Dad—"

"Lyndsey!" Simon barked. "Put them down and come here!"

The force of his voice penetrated her daze. Slowly she laid the baby Empt beside its brother—or sister. Four round yellow eyes glowed in a row. Lyndsey left the niche, slid down the slope. In amazement Rob saw her face actually change. It lost that look of blithe unconcern. It became haggard, white, fearful.

Lyndsey rubbed her temple. "What—what happened?" A glance into the darkness. She was suddenly aware again. "I forgot everything!"

"Good," said Simon. "That means that together, those little babies may be radiating at almost the level of an adult

Empt. I think we have a chance. Listen carefully, both of you. This is extremely important. Once I pick up those Empts, I'll forget everything too. I won't know what to do—or why—unless you tell me."

And in terse sentences, Simon outlined what must be done.

Rob felt a twinge of hope. He suppressed it quickly. He was all too fearful that it would prove false. Yet he paid close attention to the Commander's instructions.

"Take this." Simon passed his torch to his daughter. "Stay far enough away from me so that you don't pick up the emanations."

"Empting won't hurt you, will it, Dad?" Lyndsey wanted to know.

"No. The combined power of the babies obviously isn't as strong as that of the Empt that Rob caught in Churchill. Its power knocked him out, remember? This is a case of too little, not too much. The Empts affected you. But can they affect—Well, let's stop talking and find out."

He clumped up the slope, his boots stirring the damp sand. Rob held the torch steady. It wasn't easy. Fatigue made his hand shake.

Simon entered the niche, bent down. He picked up both baby Empts and fitted one in the crook of each arm.

One Empt shot out two pseudopods, then quickly retracted them. It settled comfortably into place with a piping *chee-wee.*

Encircled by the light from the torches, Simon stared down at Rob and his daughter. His face was smooth and untroubled.

"Come on, Commander," Rob called. "Walk down here with them."

Simon took time to evaluate the request. His grimy face had a curious air of innocence. For a moment Rob feared the strategy wouldn't work.

Then Simon lifted his right boot over the pink remains of the egg. He carried the babies down the slope.

Without speaking, Simon followed Lyndsey and Rob back beneath the suspended hull to where Footloose lay.

Despite the chill of the cave air, Rob started sweating again. Everything hung on the next few moments. Everything.

"Put the Empts down, Commander."

Simon's movements were slow, deliberate. But he obeyed. Gently he set the Empts down.

"Now take that plasto binding off the bearded man's wrist."

In a minute or so Simon had the knot free. He peered at the fibrous belt in his hand, tossed it away with a shrug.

"Roll him over on his back."

This Simon proceeded to do.

"Now shake him so he wakes up. That's it. Harder, sir."

Lyndsey gripped Rob's arm. "He's coming around."

"All right, Commander. Set the Empts on his chest and get away."

"I'm perfectly safe here," Simon returned. "There's no reason why—"

"Do it, Commander! The Empts on the man's chest. Then stand back."

Obeying but not comprehending, Simon lifted one of the squeaking babies. He set it on Footloose's heaving chest.

The bearded man was beginning to make loud snuffling sounds. He shuddered. The Empt toppled into the sand, landing on the upper curve of its spherical body. It shot three pseudopods into the air, righted itself, engaged its pseudopods in the sand and started to scuttle off.

"Catch it, Commander!" Rob's voice was raw with strain. "Take hold of it."

Simon extended his hands. He seized the baby Empt just before it raced out of range.

Under Rob's direction, Simon cradled the Empt and soothed it with a wordless murmur. Footloose was nearly awake now, thrashing his arms and groaning. His eyes opened. There was sudden memory in those eyes.

"Put the Empts on his chest, Dad!" Lyndsey cried.

Simon responded, dumping one baby Empt onto Footloose's shirt. Then he scooped the other from the sand and deposited it beside the first.

Footloose struggled to sit up. The Empt's faceted eyes were bright as yellow jewels. They squeaked steadily. Footloose gazed past them, recognizing Rob for one awful instant—

*Chee-wee, chee-wee.* The sound diverted the bearded man's attention.

He examined the Empts perched on his chest. One leathery hand crept up to touch the armor of the smaller baby. His blue eyes turned almost dreamy.

"Critters." His white teeth shone through his beard. "Critters."

"Get away, Dad," Lyndsey whispered to her father.

Rob shared her concern. "Come over by us, Commander. Hurry!"

Simon walked toward them with a stiff, stumbling gait. He stopped between Rob and his daughter. He glanced from one to the other, vacant, uncertain.

All at once his eyes cleared.

Simon pounded the palms of his hands against his eye sockets. He shook his head. Remembered. Swiftly he pivoted toward Footloose, who was gurgling and chortling over the newfound pets that squeaked on his stomach.

The Commander spoke very softly. "Footloose?"

The bearded man turned to the voice. He frowned.

"I know you, person."

Lyndsey's hand stole to her father's arm, dug in tightly. Rob fought to steady the torch he held. Simon Ling swallowed a deep gulp of air, continued in a low, earnest voice.

"Of course you know me, Footloose. The Commander of the Conpats."

"Won't hurt me? Won't hurt me, Commander person?"

"You know I won't. But I need your help, Footloose. We seem to have lost our way down in these caves."

Rob marveled at the way Simon managed to say it so casually. As if it hardly mattered.

"Can you help us find our way out, Footloose?" Simon asked.

The man started to stand up again. Both Empts tumbled off. He caught one. The other struck the ground.

Footloose picked it up, crooned over it, rubbed his beard against it. With one Empt in each arm, he frowned a second time. His blue gaze slid past the Commander to Rob.

Rob's stomach turned over. He was sure Footloose remembered him and everything else.

Footloose growled. "That person. Young person. Something bad on his face. Makes me think of bad things. There is something bad here."

He lifted his head. He searched the high darkness for the hull of *Majestica*. Mercifully, it could not be seen.

"His name is Edison person, yes?" Footloose hissed it again, almost angrily. "Edison person bad!"

"No," Simon insisted. "Forget that. He's your friend."

"Need remember why person is very bad," Footloose insisted.

"He isn't, Footloose. He's a friend. We're all your friends."

For one moment Footloose's face mirrored the awful struggle. The past fought against the obliterating power of the Empts. Rob's hand shook harder.

"We'll protect your critters if you help us," Simon offered. "You can have both of those for your own."

A blink of the blue-chip eyes.

"Both?"

"That's a promise."

Once more Footloose lifted his gaze to the darkness at the cavern roof. Slowly, he swung to Rob, and stared.

The Empt in Footloose's arm squeaked loudly. Footloose giggled. He pressed his filthy bearded cheek against the creature to quiet it.

"These are my critters, Commander person?"

"Yes."

Hesitation.

"All right."

Simon breathed with relief. Rob didn't know whether to laugh or cry or both.

Footloose bobbed his head to show that he would lead the way. Two hours later he guided them past a tunnel turning. Ahead, Rob saw a patch of sky washed with the lemon sun of Stardeep.

# Twenty-one

## "GOOD FORTUNE ACROSS STARDEEP"

"Attention. Attention, please. FTLS *Roger Dunleavy* is now in the final boarding process. All passengers holding space should be cleared through customs and aboard. Repeat, all passengers holding space should be cleared through customs and aboard. Thank you."

Rob's bubblegrip popped from beneath the last inspection scope and bumped toward the end of the moving belt. Another taped message boomed into the dome. It was less detailed than the one Rob had heard on arrival. The automated voice merely hoped that all persons boarding the FTLS had enjoyed a pleasant stay on Stardeep, and would return again.

*Fantastic would be a better word*, thought Rob. *Come back? Never.*

He carried his bubblegrip toward Simon and Lyndsey. They were waiting for him by the hatch that led into the loading pod. A purser from the *Roger Dunleavy* watched with obvious impatience. Rob was the last passenger who had to be boarded.

Three days had passed since Footloose had guided Rob and his friends out of the caves. Along with Simon and his daughter, Rob had spent one of those days undergoing exhaustive tests in the Conpat dispensary.

The tests proved negative. Massive nutritional therapy plus twelve hours of hypnotically induced rest restored Rob to some degree of normalcy. He didn't feel tired any longer. Only, only—well—changed.

In the dispensary there had been plenty of time to talk. Rob told Simon and Lyndsey everything. That included the

149

incidents with Kerry Sharkey and the question of the interview that author Hollis Kipp wanted in the fall. He had
been seven days on Stardeep. Nearly two of them had been
spent in the caves. The past had no more secrets. But the
future had problems without limit.

Simon offered no advice during the dispensary discus-
sions. He puffed on his musicpipe, putting forth a question
now and then, but refraining from any kind of opinion. It
wasn't necessary that Simon speak. Rob recalled with shining clarity what the Commander had told him during the
awful time in the caves.

But Rob hadn't yet brought himself to the point of ac-
cepting that advice. Somehow he couldn't.

"You forgot one package, Rob," Lyndsey said as he approached.

Startled, Rob lifted his bubblegrip. "This is all I have."

She shook her head. Her bright blue eyes twinkled. She
looked crisp and fresh in a white one-piece. Except for
some lingering shadows under her eyes, the experience in
the caves might never have happened.

Simon too was freshly turned out in a black Conpat uniform, the gold emblems gleaming on his shoulder. His
musicpipe gave off aromatic smoke and the second movement of a symphony composed by one of the first of the
great creative computers.

"My daughter has a somewhat illegal present for you,"
Simon observed, not pleased.

From behind her back Lyndsey brought a small plasto
shipping container. There were several ventilation ports
punched into the sides below the carry handle. Official seals
all over the surface proclaimed that the parcel had been
cleared by Stardeep customs. Puzzled, Rob also saw a
special stamp which read STARDEEP CONSERVANCY PATROL
RELEASE #11048.

"Take it, please," Lyndsey urged.

"What is it, Lyn?" he wanted to know.

With obvious disapproval Simon told him. "A baby
Empt. The container is especially shielded inside. You have
to open it for Empting. Lyndsey's idea, not mine. Let's not
go into the details of how she got it. Being the Commander's daughter unfortunately lets a girl swing weight in
some quarters where she shouldn't. I didn't find out about
it until she'd already had the Empt processed and cleared.

Lyndsey looked straight at Rob and said softly, "I

wanted you to have it. I know how bad this visit has been for you. Maybe when you need to forget, this will help."

From the ventilation ports Rob heard a faint *chee-wee*. He looked closely at the container. Emotions swept over him like a storm—doubt, longing, sorrow.

The automated voice repeated its message about the final boarding. Rob continued to stare at the container in Lyndsey's outstretched hand.

He was tempted. That package held a lifetime of forgetting.

"Rob?" Lyndsey said.

"I can't take it, Lyndsey."

Afterward he often wondered how he had reached that decision. It hadn't come consciously. Yet there it was. And he was committed to it—and all it meant—for the rest of his days.

Strangely he felt better almost at once. Simon's glance thawed. Even Lyndsey seemed pleased.

The Commander reached out, gently pried the container handle from his daughter's hand. "I made a little bet with her, Rob. I told her you wouldn't take it. People grow up in different ways and in different places. Stardeep was your place."

Rob wasn't so sure. But Simon's smile cheered him. To his discomfort, he noticed that Lyndsey was crying.

The purser at his elbow coughed impatiently. Lyndsey darted forward suddenly to kiss him on the cheek.

"I'm glad you didn't take it," she whispered.

"Your tickets, if you please," the purser said in an officious voice.

Rob handed over the punched machine forms. Simon waved his musicpipe. "Come visit us if you can, Rob."

He looked at Lyndsey. "I will."

"All in order," the purser was saying. "Into the loading pod, please, Mr. Edison."

"—and send us a beam and tell us how the exams come out," Simon finished. "Good fortune across Stardeep!"

There was much more Rob wanted to say. There was no time.

The purser followed him into the pod. The hatch slid shut. The pod disengaged and began to rise. Through a small port he saw the side of the great FTLS flashing past.

Even now he wasn't sure he understood it all. So much had happened in such a short span. The nightmare in the caves, Footloose, gone back now to his old untroubled life on the reservation with not one but two Empts, the fate of *Majestica*—

One thing was certain. It was over. He had the exams to worry about.

As the loading pod rose, he found himself facing the thought of the tests with fresh confidence. In fact, everything looked much brighter.

He still wasn't sure that he could wholly accept the truth about Lightcommander Edison. On Stardeep he had learned —painfully—that his father was a human being subject to error. Somehow it was an ordeal to think of Duncan Edison that way.

Yet when he did so consciously, as now, a bit of the burden seemed to lift from his shoulders.

He thought briefly of Lyndsey's offered gift. By taking it, he would never have needed to fret about the secrets buried in the ground of Stardeep. Never for the rest of his life.

But as the boarding pod decelerated, it struck him that, had he taken the Empt, he would never have remembered his father either.

Rob stowed his bubblegrip away in the tiny cabin. Then he strapped himself into his slingbunk. Bells rang. The intercall announced launch in sixty seconds. The great thrusters boomed.

Rob turned his head to the small port. Smoke boiled and blew. The pressure of acceleration squeezed against his chest. He had a last glimpse of the planet through the tatters of vapor—windy wasteland, purple crags, the geodesics of Churchill aglow in the lemon sun.

Then the curve of Stardeep's horizon defined itself. The color of the atmosphere darkened. The thrusters cut out. The port opaqued, crawling with magenta light.

Presently Rob unstrapped himself. He opened his bubblegrip. He took out the small platinum-framed fax of his father.

*C.D.E.*, he forced himself to say in his mind. *C.D.E., but so what?*

Empting would have been wrong. In fact, a lot of the past had been wrong.

Not that facing the truth was easy. But he had made his decision when Lyndsey offered the Empt. He had to live with the truth. That was the last of Stardeep's secrets.

*All right,* he said to himself. *Follow that where it leads. Living with the truth means facing Kerry Sharkey.*

*It won't be easy. But I can do it.*

*What about giving Hollis Kipp an interview?*

*I have to.*

Was this what Simon Ling meant by growing up? Perhaps he could be himself now. Rob Edison, student. Not some extension of himself forever living in the past.

Rob smiled at the fax. Really smiled. And he realized another surprising thing.

He loved his father.

How long had it been since he had looked at the fax without feeling resentment and fear? How long had it been since he had looked at that fax with a smile on his face instead of a knot in his middle?

Too long.

He laughed.

It was a wonderful feeling.

## About the Author

John Jakes was born in Chicago. He is a graduate of DePauw University and took his M.A. in literature at Ohio State. He sold his first short story during his second year of college, and his first book twelve months later. Since then, he has published more than 200 short stories and over 50 books—suspense, nonfiction, science fiction, and historical novels. His novels comprising the American Bicentennial Series were all bestsellers, and his books have appeared in translation from Europe to Japan. Originally intending to become an actor, Mr. Jakes' continuing interest in the theater has manifested itself in four plays and the books and lyrics for five musicals, all of which are currently in print and being performed by stock and amateur groups around the United States. The author is married, the father of four children, and lists among his organizations the Authors Guild, the Dramatists Guild, and Science Fiction Writers of America. In 1976 he was awarded an honorary doctorate by Wright State University for his contribution to the nation's Bicentennial observance. His science fiction novel, *Time Gate,* is also available in a Signet edition.